PRAISE FOR
QUIM MONZÓ

"A gifted writer, he draws well on the rich tradition of Spanish surrealism to put a deliberately paranoic sense of menace in the apparently mundane everyday and also to sustain the lyrical, visionary quality of his imagination."

—*New York Times*

"Quim Monzó is today's best known writer in Catalan. He is also, no exaggeration, one of the world's great short-story writers. . . . We have at last gained the opportunity to read (in English) one of the most original writers of our time."

—*The Independent* (London)

"To read *The Enormity of the Tragedy* is to enter a fictional universe created by an author trapped between aversion to and astonishment at the world in which he has found himself. His almost manic humor is underpinned by a frighteningly bleak vision of daily life."

—*Times Literary Supplement* (London)

GUADALAJARA

STORIES BY

QUIM MONZÓ

TRANSLATED FROM THE CATALAN BY PETER BUSH

Copyright © 1996, 1999 by Joaquim Monzó
Copyright © 1996, 1999 by Quaderns Crema, S. A.
Translation copyright © 2011 by Peter Bush
Published by arrangement with Quaderns Crema, S. A., 2008
First published in Catalan as *Guadalajara*, by Quaderns Crema, S. A., 1996

First edition, 2011

Library of Congress Cataloging-in-Publication Data:

Monzó, Quim, 1952-
    [Guadalajara. English]
    Guadalajara : stories / by Quim Monzó ; translated from the
Catalan by Peter Bush. — 1st ed.
      p. cm.
    First published in Catalan as Guadalajara, in 1996.
    ISBN-13: 978-1-934824-19-1 (pbk. : alk. paper)
    ISBN-10: 1-934824-19-4 (pbk. : alk. paper)
  1. Monzó, Quim, 1952—Translations into English.
  I. Bush, Peter R., 1946- II. Title.

    PC3942.23.O53G8313 2011
    849'.9354—dc22

                  2011008812

Translation of this novel was made possible thanks to the
support of the Ramon Llull Institut.

LLLL institut
ramon llull
Catalan Language and Culture

Printed on acid-free paper in the United States of America.

Text set in FF Scala, a serif typeface designed by Martin Majoor in 1990
for the Vredenburg Music Center in Utrecht, the Netherlands.

Design by N. J. Furl

Open Letter is the University of Rochester's nonprofit, literary translation press:
Lattimore Hall 411, Box 270082, Rochester, NY 14627

www.openletterbooks.org

Contents

1.

Family Life   5

2.

Outside the Gates of Troy   21
Helvetian Freedoms   25
Gregor   31
A Hunger and Thirst for Justice   37

3.

A Day Like Any Other   47
Life Is So Short   51
The Power of Words   56
Literature   61

4.

Centripetal Force   67

5.

Strategies   85
The Lives of the Prophets   96
During the War   113
Books   120

"They began slowly, then picked up speed."

—Gustave Flaubert, *Madame Bovary*

I

Family
Life

Armand ran into the workshop, making an engine noise with his mouth and stamping on the wood shavings on the floor so they crackled underfoot: the louder the better. He walked twice around the carpenter's bench; looked at all the tools perfectly aligned on the wall, the saws, gouges, clamps and planes, each in their rightful place (marked by a suitable outline, roughly penciled in); and went up the passageway at the rear of which the house, properly speaking, began. Uncle Reguard had put his workshop in the back of his house, and although the grown-ups always entered through the front door, Armand preferred to go in via the workshop. He was fascinated by the fact that his uncle's workplace was right at the back of his house. In contrast, he lived in an apartment, and his father's carpentry workshop occupied a ground-floor space four blocks from where they lived. His cousins had a similar set up. Uncle Reguard was the only member of the family to have his workshop and home together; separated by a small bedroom, that now acted as a junk room. If you came from the workshop, you then reached the parlor with the big table, chandelier, armchairs, passages, and bedroom doors.

By the time Armand reached the parlor everyone was already there kissing, laughing, chatting, raising their voices to make themselves heard: his father, uncles and aunts, and more distant uncles, aunts, and cousins, who weren't cousins at all and were only described as such because they belonged to branches of the family so remote they didn't know what precise labels to give them.

They ate lunch, a meal that lasted hours, and then the post-lunch conversations started, when the smoke from the cigars began to curl around everything. Empty champagne bottles piled up in the room between the house and workshop, the aunts kept slicing cake, and the older cousins put records on the turntable. The atmosphere was heavy with the aroma of hot chocolate. The young cousins (Armand, Guinovarda, Gisela, Guitart, and Llopart . . .) asked permission to leave the table and ran to Eginard's bedroom to play with wooden houses that had roofs, doors, and windows painted in a range of colors. When the bedroom door was half open, Armand could see the harp in the corner of the passage. It was a harp Uncle Reguard had built thirty years ago, and it was one of the family's prized possessions, because (so Armand's father would say) he had combined carpentry with the art of crafting string instruments. For as long as he could remember, Armand had seen the harp at Uncle Reguard's and always in the same place: in the corner made by the bend in the passage. He thought it was more beautiful than all the harps in the photographs and drawings that he'd cut out from magazines (and kept in a blue folder at home): a harp in the hands of a mythological god, a Sumerian harp topped by the head of an animal he couldn't identify, the Irish coat-of-arms, two Norwegian harps (one topped by a dragon's head and the other by the head of a blind-folded woman), and a harp made from a tree branch that Harpo Marx was plucking.

•

Cousin Reguard came into the bedroom, crying and smiling, in the midst of cheering adults. His right hand was holding a chocolate and peppermint ice cream, and his left hand was bandaged. It was a scene Armand had often seen in these family get-togethers, whether they were held in their home, their cousins', or the homes of other more distant cousins, some of who even lived in other cities. A boy would appear with a bandaged left hand. The bandage was always wrapped around his ring finger. Armand knew there was no longer a finger under the bandage, and that the bandage would eventually fall away, revealing a tiny, perfectly healed stump. Armand surveyed the hands of his family. As he'd registered some time ago, everyone over nine was missing the ring finger of their left hand.

Armand was seven when he first realized it was no accident that one of the boys would always leave the party with his ring finger cut off. He'd not really paid much attention till now. It was true he'd noticed the older kids were missing that finger, but it was a completely normal state of affairs for him. It had never been any different. He thought the absence must be synonymous with adult life. Every adult in the family lost that finger for a reason that eluded him and that didn't concern him one little bit. So many things eluded him—he knew he wouldn't understand them until he became an adult, and he didn't worry about a trifle that was quite unimportant when compared to the other issues that preoccupied him at the time: the spirit of sacrifice displayed by St. Bernard dogs, the origins of existence, or the offside trap in football. As he saw it, in order to hit adolescence and abandon the world of little kids, he too would have to lose his ring finger. He thought it was understandable, normal, and desirable, like losing his milk teeth.

When he started to go to school, he was surprised to see how many adults had four fingers and a thumb on each hand, as if *that* were completely normal. He thought theirs was a surprising, eccentric, and rather unpleasant circumstance, and he was proud to belong to such a consistent family. As the months passed, and he spent more time in the company of other kids, he started to think that perhaps the members of his family experienced random accidents and that these accidents always led to the loss of the ring finger. The boy he shared a desk with at school told him it was quite common for carpenters to lose fingers. The carpenter near his house (he went on) was missing three. His mother had told him it happened to lots of carpenters, because one day or another the blade of the circular saw would slice a finger off. Armand knew that wasn't the case in his family. They were carpenters, but it wasn't the circular saw that sliced off their fingers, or any other accident. At the age of nine, the kids weren't yet carpenters and didn't even know that's what they wanted to be when they grew up; even though from time immemorial all the members of his family had showed an undeniable inclination towards that trade, and apart from a few exceptional cases, they invariably ended up as carpenters.

Armand spent his nights ruminating about this mystery. Perhaps there was a guild rule that obliged them to chop off that finger? He reached a conclusion he wasn't sure how to verify: they chopped that first finger off to get them used to the idea. Losing that first finger meant they lost their fear of the possible loss of others. They realized it wasn't such a big deal; it gave them courage and helped them tackle their trade with true valor. One thing sent his head into a whirl: he'd met the father of a school friend, from another class, who also happened to be a carpenter, and none of his fingers were missing (he used to take a look whenever he picked up his son at the end of the school day).

•

As the adults didn't consider it a tragedy, and seemed particularly happy at the exact moment when the finger disappeared (especially the parents of the boy whose finger was amputated), Armand didn't find it tragic either. Until that afternoon two years ago, when he became conscious for the first time that, on whatever day of the year a member of the family celebrated a ninth birthday, they lost that finger, and it would be his fate too; he felt frightened that afternoon. He was with his cousins in the bedroom, playing with those wooden houses. Eginard, Gisela, and Gimfreu had all had that finger chopped off. Llopart and he still retained all four fingers, and that meant they were still kids. When Eginard got up from their game, Armand went over to him, swallowed, and asked him what the finger business was all about. Llopart, Gisela, and Gimfreu all looked around for a moment, then went back to the game they were playing, going in and out of the houses. Eginard asked him to repeat the question, perhaps to get more time to think up his reply. Armand expanded his question: What was the finger thing all about? They'd cut off little Reguard's today; they cut a finger off from everyone, one day or another, when they reached the age of nine. Llopart looked at them all, clueless. Eginard got up, stroked Armand's head, and dragged him gently out of the bedroom. Armand wouldn't relent: Why was everyone in their family missing the same finger on their left hand, a finger people outside their family kept? Armand scrutinized Eginard's finger; it had been chopped off at the metacarpus—a clean scar from a perfect strike.

And why the ring finger on the left hand and not the little finger on the right, or an index finger? Was it some hygienic measure, the reason for which had been forgotten with the passage of time? He just couldn't understand. It was evident it was an ancestral custom, but how had it originated? Had they practiced it for centuries? Or simply decades? On his ninth birthday, his father found him crying in bed.

"I don't want my finger chopped off."

"What an odd thing to say!"

"I want to be normal, like the other kids at school."

"Being normal has nothing to do with having one finger more or one less."

His father wiped away his tears and told him that normal is a cultural value and consequently completely relative; some people like crew-cuts, others like long hair, some prefer a beard and mustache, some only a mustache and others only a beard, and some even shave the whole lot off; there are nations where both men and women depilate themselves and others where only the women do. We cut our toenails, and that's precisely what makes us different from animals and primitive peoples who prefer to keep them very long. Armand disagreed with these comparisons. Hair and nails grow again, fingers don't. The sun was shining through the window; father and son looked at the warm lines the beams were tracing on the ground.

"You don't have to make your mind up immediately."

"I've already made it up, and I don't want to do it."

"Why not?"

"You can't play the harp if you're a finger short."

•

He surprised even himself. He'd said that quite spontaneously. Nevertheless, although he'd not realized that or thought about it before, it was out in the open, his father was in the know, and it could very well be true that he wanted to be a harpist, so he kept to his story. Months ago he'd seen a television report about Nicanor Zabaleta playing the harp, and it was quite obvious he needed all his fingers. A harpist needed every single one. His father was looking at him solemnly. He'd never seen him so solemn.

"If you like music, there are lots of different instruments. It doesn't have to be a harp."

"But I like the harp."

"You're just obsessed with the harp at your uncle's. But the world of musical instruments doesn't stop at the harp. Just think how many others there are: the kettledrum, the bass drum, the tambourine, the bongo, the triangle . . ." Armand stared at him, betraying no sign of excitement at these possibilities. "Perhaps you think the maracas are small potatoes, but what about the drums? Drums give lots of scope: the bass drum, the ordinary drum, the tom-tom, the cymbals and the snare. And never forget the xylophone!"

Armand spent the next few months in a very jumpy state. The belief had always circulated in the family (always mentioned jokingly) that they'd cut a kid's finger off one day, but it would grow back with time. Some said it would be a sign that something was about to happen, but they never got around to saying exactly what. Others said that, in effect, the finger would grow back but that this would mean nothing in particular. That story sowed fresh doubts in Armand's mind: What if he refused to let them chop his finger off and he was the chosen one whose finger would grow back after it had been removed? What an absurd situation! His refusal would prevent that miracle from ever happening.

He was obsessed by fingers. He noticed how some people wore a ring on the ring finger of their left hand. In his family, nobody had a ring finger, so they always wore it on the little finger, and when it came to the marriage ceremony, the priest always looked on impassively when the time came for the bride and bridegroom to put their rings on. Armand once saw a complete stranger in the street who was missing the ring finger of his left hand, and he spent days investigating whether he was a distant relative, so distant he didn't even know him. Perhaps other families shared the same tradition. Or similar

ones? Perhaps they amputated other fingers, or other parts of the body
. . . but why? What sense did it make? And what did they do with the
fingers they'd chopped off? Did they bury them? Armand imagined
them buried vertically, like asparagus shoots, in small graveyards for
fingers. Perhaps they cremated them.

He gradually started to see his parents and the rest of his relatives
through different eyes. What kind of macabre tradition were they
cherishing; how could they go along with it so pitilessly? As he didn't
trust them, he slept with his left hand under the pillow where he rest-
ed his head. He'd calculated that it would be quite impossible for them
to lift up his head, remove the pillow, take his hand out, and slice his
finger off without waking him up. He would sometimes dream that,
despite all these precautions, his parents (their faces glowing sancti-
moniously) managed to lift up his head and pillow, extract his hand,
and chop off his finger with a single deft slice of the carving knife.

·

He had a panic attack when he discovered there would be a family
reunion the following Sunday. For the first time he was a candidate
to lose a finger. He and Guitard were the two most likely cousins.
Both were now nine years old. He had been nine for three months,
Guitard for seven. If seniority was an issue, it was Guitard's turn. But
amputations weren't always carried out according to the principle of
seniority, and that meant it could very well be his turn this time.

Sunday came, and they didn't chop off his finger, or Guitard's, but
Teodard's, a cousin who had a month to go before his ninth birthday;
theoretically, they should have left him intact. Guitard was furious.
He was up for the chop and *not* that cousin. They told him why they'd
moved Teodard forward: his mother was pregnant, so they'd wanted
to get the whole business over and done with—when the new baby

arrived, there'd be no need to worry about the big brother's finger. Armand was intrigued by Guitard's attitude. He asked him if he wasn't shocked by the idea of having his finger chopped off. Why should he be? On the contrary, he couldn't see what the problem was and was shocked Armand even asked the question.

"They aren't chopping your neck off. It's only a finger, and not even the most important one at that."

Guitard was crazy about becoming a grown up. Consequently, at the next family reunion, he ran into the room where the other kids were playing with toy trains, proudly waving his bandaged finger.

•

When the new cousin was born (they called him Abelard), there was a big fuss, whispered exchanges, and sudden silences whenever a youngster entered a bedroom. All the secrecy aroused Armand's curiosity. But he found out only three days later that Abelard had been born with five fingers and a thumb on his left hand.

The whole family was alarmed. What would they do when Abelard made it to nine? If they chopped one finger off, he would have eight, not seven like everybody else. According to some, this might be seen as an offensive point of comparison, and two should be chopped off so he was like the rest of the family. Conversely, others thought it would be excessive to cut two off, if they cut off only one from everybody else. Only one should be amputated. This is what they'd always done, and there was no reason to start changing their tradition. The debates followed various tangents, got very involved, and always came back to square one. Finally, they reached the obvious conclusion: this was an exceptional case and, as such, merited an exceptional solution. Besides, there was no need to rush things. Abelard wouldn't be nine for years, and that's when the decision should be taken.

This reconciliatory conclusion fell flat, however, a few weeks later when cousin Gerarda was born: she also had an extra finger, and it was also on her left hand. So Abelard's case was no longer exceptional, and the first serious doubts began to appear. It made no sense to delay a decision until Abelard and Gerarda were nine. A stenotypist uncle, a jazz fan, dared to ask what the point was in continuing with the whole tradition. It was the provocation they were all waiting for. The family reacted as one. An immemorial legacy couldn't be questioned simply because of the random occurrence of two babies being born with five-fingered left hands. The dissident was told his question was out of order, and with a great sense of purpose, a date was fixed for their next reunion: a month later, at the beginning of December.

Within the week, however, news came from Barbastre of a third cousin's birth (quite a distant one): five fingers. It suddenly became clear that speaking of random occurrences was inappropriate and that delaying a decision for nine years resolved nothing. Some family members argued there was no cause for alarm; the fact that children in the family were being born with five fingers on one hand was the consequence of a logical process of evolution. Even Uncle Reguard speculated that so many centuries (some spoke of millennia) of cutting off ring fingers had finally led to a mutation: babies in the family were being born with an extra finger in order to compensate for the one they'd lose at the age of nine. Other family members thought that his opinion was absurd and refused to accept there could be such a significant mutation after a few centuries, or even a few millennia. In fact, it didn't matter who was right. For the first time, there was a deep schism in the family that threatened their harmony. On the one side, there were those who believed two fingers should be chopped off of children with five-fingered left hands (the ring finger, as usual, and this new intermediate finger between the ring finger and middle finger that doesn't have a special name) and there was no need to wait until they were nine: it should be done immediately, in a show of strength, to stamp out any dissent. On the other, there were those who believed that, if the tradition was to cut off one finger, however many anatomical variants there might be, they should continue being loyal to tradition and only chop one finger off. A third opinion appeared in the heat of the debate, initially a minority view, defended by the stenotypist uncle and two sisters-in-law: they denounced the custom itself as barbaric.

•

It was particularly significant that the sisters-in-law had denounced the practice—after becoming convinced during their courtship, people who married into the family had always turned into the most enthusiastic champions of the rite. In fact, one of the culminating moments in the festivities (and the source of perennial leg-pulling in family reunions) was when, if relationships looked rock-solid, a member of the family would address their future partner, saying he must tell her something before their betrothal could be ratified. It was an act that would initially seem strange, though it wasn't at all, and their joint future as a married couple depended on a proper understanding of the tradition. And then they would go on to say, "When our children turn nine, we chop the ring finger off their left hand."

The idea would always meet with reticence (as if it were a kind of joke) and immediately after (when it was realized it was no joke) with horror. The objections were always the same: "How can you do something so barbaric in this day and age?", "What's the point?", "You're not going to do that to *our* children!" Then the persuasion process began, hours of conversation and arguments. Day after day refining, clarifying, stressing until the future spouse finally understood. From that point on they became the most ardent champions of the act, and (although, in principle, nobody asked them to do this) they surrendered their own ring fingers, so they could fully enter into the spirit of the family. They were also the first to demand the rite be carried out when the child was nine, with no holds barred, and volunteered to keep the child's hand still.

That was why revisionism from that quarter of the family, from the converts who seemingly clung to the custom most, was so serious. But this consideration gradually ceased to be important; soon there were no distinctions, and everyone joined the initial caucus formed by the stenotypist and the two sisters-in-law. A fourth cousin was born with five fingers. Everything now escalated to a crisis-point: people began to distance themselves, and the reunion arranged for the beginning of December was postponed *sine die*. "Until a final decision is reached." But many assumed this was simply a way to get them out of the fix and intuited that there never would be a final decision, apart from that declaration, which apparently wasn't one.

•

They bought a harp for Armand and signed him up for music and harp lessons on Tuesdays and Thursdays after school. He practiced conscientiously and assiduously on the weekends, but it didn't always show in performance. As it became clear the family custom of chopping off fingers was now a thing of the past, Armand's desire to play the harp gradually waned, and the next year, the harp stayed in a corner accumulating dust, until years later when Elisard, one of his five-fingered cousins, took an interest. Whenever there was a family lunch at Armand's (now they were lucky to have seven or eight relatives when before twenty or more always came), Elisard would go into Armand's bedroom and play the harp. Every get-together he played better. Until in the end he was playing compositions by Halffter, Milhaud, and Ginastera, and (a family special request) songs from Paraguay, and a Mexican tune he kept encoring ever more zestfully. Armand's parents suggested giving him the harp as a gift. Armand interpreted that as a hint (as a reproach, after he'd defended his vocation as a harpist so energetically and then shown so little interest). He saw no point in pandering to them and said he couldn't care less what they did with it. His parents decided to present it to Elisard the next time he visited.

But Elisard never returned to Armand's. Without the cohesive element of the ceremony, family reunions became more and more infrequent; less people went to the few that were held, and soon everyone found an excuse not to go: in winter, people had to go skiing; in the summer, to the beach; and in any season of the year there was always some commitment that couldn't be cancelled. Within a few years, family reunions were ancient history, and even the closest relatives became strangers they spoke to once a year at most, and then on the phone.

Elisard was the only one everyone still had news of, because over time (some say it had to do with his small anatomical extra) he turned into an exceptional harpist, who restored to the instrument the prestige and high standing it had lost as a result of being little played for many years. Armand thought differently. He thought Elisard was a child prodigy who'd enjoyed a few years as a star but, as he got older, he cut a pathetic figure: he, his harp, and his mannered melodies. Now, as he leaned on the bar, Armand saw Elisard yet again on the TV next to the shelves of bottles. He looked around, swore at the top of his voice and advocated the need to reinstate the old custom of chopping off ring fingers, starting with that famous harpist's. The others propping up the bar don't even look at him. As they don't listen to him, he recounts the story of his family. Two patrons who do finally pay him some attention decide he's either mad or drunk, or both things at once. Only one girl seems to take a positive interest, and she sidles over when he stops talking. She is pretty and has a lovely smile and a lock of brown hair that hides half of her face, the way some women hide a glass eye.

2

Outside the Gates of Troy

The wooden horse was finally completed, polished and varnished, at the break of day. It had been hard work and required dozens of soldiers supervised by three master carpenters. Majestic and motionless, it rises above the centre of the beach. They leave it to dry the whole day. At night, watching carefully to ensure nobody can see them from the wall, the chosen warriors climb quickly up a hemp ladder, one after another, making no noise. They are armed with small bags, filled with salted meat to give them strength in the morning and a ration of water to slake their thirst, are tied to their belts. After the last warrior has climbed up, they pull in the ladder and close the door so it isn't visible from the outside.

They sit down in an orderly, patient manner, packed together in the belly of the beast. The smell of varnish lingers on inside and intoxicates them all. They sleep lightly, nervous on the eve of an imminent victory. As agreed, at dawn, the soldiers in the encampment will collect their belongings, set fire to the tents, and board their ships, thus demonstrating that they have abandoned the war as lost and are making a definitive retreat. The chosen warriors watch their movements through the cracks between the timber planks. When the Achaean ships disappear over the horizon, they turn their gaze on the gates of the city. Soon they will open, the Trojans will emerge, take possession of the horse as war booty, and trundle it inside. The Achaean warriors use the wait to eat the meat they'd brought with them.

The hours pass slowly and nobody leaves the city. Ulysses orders the first soldier to express surprise to shut up. Nobody must open his mouth, and they must all make as little noise as possible. If a Trojan emerges and hears men speaking inside the horse, then all their guile will have been in vain.

By early afternoon they've drunk all the water they had left. The belly of the horse is like an oven under the relentless sun. At night they sleep and don't feel cold. They are so many and so tightly packed together there's no room to spread a blanket. The real problem is their pee. They've spent the whole previous day and night inside, and some decide to urinate on the sly in the various corners because they can't hold it anymore. But the needs of Anticles are major rather than minor. Ulysses orders him to hold it. Anticles says he can't (his stomach's all knotted, he can't resist a single moment more), and he loses his nerve and complains that the Trojans ought to have rolled the horse inside by now. They shouldn't have to spend so long in there. He blurts this out: Ulysses has to strangle him to shut him up.

Their hopes are renewed when dawn breaks. The Trojans will definitely come today, finally take the horse and push it inside. It was only to be expected they wouldn't do it yesterday, because they still must have been suspicious. They'll do it today, as it is obvious the Achaeans have gone for good. This is confirmed mid-morning when they hear music coming from the city, strange songs that are undeniably cheerful. They must be celebrating their victory. In the afternoon the Trojans finally open the city gates. The Achaean warriors are jubilant and (excited yet keeping still so as not to make a sound) watch a group of Trojans leaving the city and walking over to the horse. The Achaeans hold their breath. The Trojans surround the wooden animal and look at it, intrigued. They discuss it amongst themselves, but, although they listen hard, the Achaeans can't hear what they are saying. They hear the murmur of voices blend with the sound of waves. Now at last they'll take the horse and push it inside. But rather than do that they retrace their steps, go back inside, and close the gates.

The Achaeans find that night the most difficult one to get to sleep. They are all hungry and thirsty. They have no food or water left, and no way to get any, and that means there are frequent arguments that Ulysses cuts dead: he doesn't want to hear a single sound. Or snore. The slightest noise could alert the Trojans to their ploy. Dawn breaks. The day passes and nobody comes. Ulysses hides his own concern. The rest of the warriors don't. They're hungry, and someone is complaining all the time that it's not going to plan. Ulysses threatens to strangle anyone who won't shut up.

Two days later two warriors suggest leaving the horse, come what may, even if doing so reveals their ruse to the Trojans. It's clear, they say, that it hasn't worked, and only idiots persist with a plan that's not working. Ulysses suppresses the attempted mutiny as he'd threatened to: by strangling them as he strangled Anticles. As they haven't eaten for days, the warriors devour both corpses. One warrior, whose stomach is too delicate, vomits at the first bite. They all decide to drink their own urine in order to stave off dehydration.

The stink from the urine and excrement is heightened by the stench from the first corpse (Anticle's, which is beginning to decompose in the heat) and from the guts of the other two. Someone suggests getting rid of them by opening the door and throwing them out. Ulysses is exasperated. How could they suggest such a thing? How could they throw them out without arousing the suspicions of the Trojans? If they left three corpses (two reduced to a pile of bones and viscera) next to the horse's hoofs, it would obviously give them away. Another warrior suggests getting rid of them at night: lower them down the ladder and throw them into the sea. Yet another opines that the worst of it isn't cohabiting with the stench from the corpses and the excrement, but the uncertainty about the future. The Achaeans must send lookouts everyday to see if the wooden horse had entered Troy, as they'd anticipated. They wouldn't leave it many more days before they recognized that their ruse had failed and sailed home, accepting total defeat. That's if they haven't done so already. Ulysses throws himself at this individual, but he has no strength left and, as they can't wrestle without any energy, they both fall on top of the other warriors who are jammed together side by side, getting thinner and thinner and weaker and weaker. Some are so still it's difficult to be sure they're still alive. Ulysses himself feels he is fainting, but he can't let that happen. The Trojans, he repeats less and less wholeheartedly, will emerge at any moment and lead the horse off. It's a matter of patience. When that happens, they (the best warriors, chosen from the *crème de la crème* of the Achaean youth) will wait until nightfall, leave the horse when the Trojans are all sleeping, sack the city, and knock its gates down. He looks longingly at the city walls through the cracks between the planks and covers his ears so he can't hear the groans of his dying warriors.

Helvetian Freedoms

O nce again the son asks his father to tell him the same old story: exactly how grandfather placed the apple on his head, how he could agree without shaking with fear, and if it really was true that he wasn't at all afraid. Walter Tell has often heard his son ask these questions. When he was a child and grandfather was still alive, it was Grandfather William who told the story. He would say that one day he went to Aldorf with his son, Walter, and in the main square they discovered that the Austrian governor, Gessler de Brunock, had decreed that everyone taking a stroll there must bow reverentially in front of a pole that was adorned with one of his hats (symbolizing himself and Greater Austria); he refused, they were arrested, and Gessler de Brunock ordered him to be hung. Walter praised his father's skill with the crossbow and Gessler de Brunock had an idea: he would test his skill by placing an apple on the child's head, and William Tell would have to hit it from eighty paces. If he hit it, he would save his own life. If he didn't, he would die.

As a child, the grandson was full of wonder at his grandfather's skill and his father's courage in submitting to such a test so readily. Consequently, whenever he told the story, he would ask whether (if only for a thousandth of a second) he'd been afraid the arrow might hit an inch too low and penetrate his son's forehead. He imagined the arrowhead sinking into his flesh, shattering his skull, and the immediate gush of blood drenching his eyes. He never imagined the other possible outcomes: the arrow going too high and getting lodged in the tree, a few inches above the apple. Or veering to the right or to the left, missing the tree trunk completely and ending up lost somewhere. He thought the first of these possible errors the most likely: William Tell would unconsciously aim too high for fear of hitting his son's forehead. Of course it was possible that he might lower his aim slightly, to counter this tendency, and that might also make him miss.

In such a situation, Walter Tell's son would have hesitated. Not because of lack of confidence in his father, but because nobody, not even the best crossbowman, could be sure to aim straight when he felt all that pressure on him. Walter Tell repeated that he'd not felt afraid at any point. How could he ever doubt his father, the man who, precisely as a result of that feat, would be transformed into the national hero? Walter Tell stroked his son's head and didn't mention that, with the passage of time, the heroic deed would finally turn into a headache. Not at the time, because he was only a child. And he wasn't lying when he said he wasn't afraid, even for a thousandth of a second, that his father wouldn't hit the apple. It was later on, when he grew up, that he began to think back and ask the questions his son now asked him. At the time of the heroic deed he was too young to grasp the real danger implicit in that challenge, but his father was no child. How could he have imperiled his son's life without shaking at all? Didn't his pulse race for a split second? What initially looked like confidence in hitting his target seemed in the end to be an indication of indifference. If he had had the shakes, if only for a moment, it would have meant, if only for the briefest moment, that he was afraid of missing and, thus, suffering for his sake. By virtue of turning it over in his mind so much, he concluded that his father didn't, in fact, love him very much. It was evident he was the best crossbowman, but he only had to be an inch off and the arrow would have shattered his skull rather than the apple. With the passage of time, and this growing awareness, Walter Tell started to become quite prickly. Every night he dreamed the arrow was flying straight at him. He was standing against the tree trunk, head erect and still, to ensure that the apple (a pippin with a delicious aroma) didn't fall. Facing him, a whole lot of people: Gessler de Brunock, several soldiers, and, among them, his father aiming his crossbow at him. Suddenly (time and again, effortlessly), the arrow (first small and distant, then suddenly huge) almost combing his hair, the squirsh of the apple shattering, and the *sshsthud* as the arrow penetrates the tree trunk. But, every now and then, in his dream the arrow hits him and not the apple. Walter would wake up, sit up, and scream in terror. His mother ran to soothe him. "It's only a nightmare, Walter, try to get back to sleep." While his mother hugged him, Walter could hear his father snoring in the matrimonial bed.

As a young man Walter Tell belonged for years to an anarchist group that was fighting for the abolition of the Swiss state. They read Bakunin, published a clandestine magazine, sang songs from countries that were on the road to development (particularly the Latin American sort), and, drunk on beer, painted circles on the walls of Freiburg University, where he studied Romance philology and was a member of the Olympic crossbow team. Years later he graduated, returned home, began living off the family inheritance, and finally devoted himself entirely to the two great passions in his life: crossbows and beer. He married the girlfriend he'd had from his first year at school. They had a child. They called the child William because that's what his wife wanted (she was a big admirer of her father-in-law) and decided to bring him up according to the pedagogical precepts of non-violence.

•

Little William admired his father and grandfather, and when he asked them to tell him the story yet again (how exactly grandfather placed the apple on his son's head, how he could agree to it without shaking with fear, if it were true he wasn't at all afraid), he felt incredibly uplifted. He felt deep, unqualified admiration for his father and grandfather. But as an adolescent, he began to feel that natural rebellion towards his father, and he'd ask in a falsetto voice (to annoy him): "Father, tell me again exactly how grandfather placed the apple on your head. How could you let him do that? Did you really not feel scared?" He uses almost the same words as before. But now his tone is mocking, and he particularly likes asking in front of his schoolfriends, so (apart from admiring him as William Tell's grandchild and the son of the child who wasn't afraid when he became a target) they now admire him because he doesn't idealize them. As far as he is concerned, those heroic figures are simply father and grandfather, like any of his friends' fathers and grandfathers. That's why he adopts the falsetto tone: "Father, tell me again exactly how grandfather placed the apple on your head. How could you let him do that? Did you really not feel scared?"

Walter Tell downs his beer, picks up his crossbow, and goes into the garden to practice. He is a good crossbowman. He has always lived in his father's shadow; however, now that he's in his forties, he can say, without arrogance, that he's even better than his father was at the same age. If they competed side by side now, he would win. That's why he finds his son's constant taunts so irksome. Not so much because he reproaches him for trusting his father (that might simply be an expression of envy), but because of his doubt: in a similar situation, would his son trust him as he'd trusted his father? Today, between one jar of beer and another, he hears his son taunting him yet again: "Father, tell me again how exactly grandfather placed the apple on your head. How could you let him do that? Did you really not feel scared?"

Walter stares at him long and hard and asks if he wouldn't like to have a try. To find out what things are like; there is nothing like experiencing it yourself, or so they say. You can get an approximate idea of what things are like from what people tell you, but you never really know what they're like until you experience them for yourself. If he places the apple on his head, he will shoot from his crossbow. No need to be afraid: he knows he is as good as his grandfather.

His son looks surprised and smiles. His father continues: if there's no reason to do it, the glory is even greater. As he speaks, he takes big strides around his son. Doing it in front of the Austrian governor, he says, added a heroic element, and the risk wasn't entirely selfless: in the long run, every heroic deed earns its own reward. On the contrary, they are quite alone in their garden and there's no heroic element involved. It's simply an issue of trust. Does he or doesn't he trust his father? He places the apple on his head, leans against the tree, and stands still.

Seen from this point of view, young William Tell is in complete agreement: accepting such a challenge has more (if not heroic) merit. It is random. Because, in fact, if he accepts it is simply to demonstrate that all the taunts he keeps making are no more than that, and if he continues to make them, knowing that deep down they hurt, it is because he wants to feel more grown up, more distanced from his father and his world of heroes of the fatherland. But deep, deep down, wouldn't he too like to join that world of heroes? To accept his father's suggestion will be even more audacious. He will surpass them both at a single stroke, because his courage is anonymous and he isn't seeking a reward. If he accepts the challenge, it will immediately make an adult of him. He runs into the kitchen, grabs an apple, goes back into the garden, looks for a tree that is eighty paces away, leans against the trunk, and places the apple on his head while his father draws his crossbow.

Gregor

When the beetle emerged from his larval state one morning, he found he had been transformed into a fat boy. He was lying on his back, which was surprisingly soft and vulnerable, and if he raised his head slightly, he could see his pale, swollen belly. His extremities had been drastically reduced in number, and the few he could feel (he counted four eventually) were painfully tender and fleshy and so thick and heavy he couldn't possibly move them around.

What *had* happened? The room seemed really tiny and the smell much less mildewy than before. There were hooks on the wall to hang a broom and mop on. In one corner, two buckets. Along another wall, a shelf with sacks, boxes, pots, a vacuum cleaner, and, propped against that, the ironing board. How small all those things seemed now—he'd hardly been able to take them in at a glance before. He moved his head. He tried twisting to the right, but his gigantic body weighed too much and he couldn't. He tried a second time, and a third. In the end he was so exhausted that he was forced to rest.

He opened his eyes again in dismay. What about his family? He twisted his head to the left and saw them, an unimaginable distance away, motionless, observing him, in horror and in fear. He was sorry they felt frightened: if at all possible, he would have apologized for the distress he was causing. Every fresh attempt he made to budge and move towards them was more grotesque. He found it particularly difficult to drag himself along on his back. His instinct told him that if he twisted on to his front he might find it easier to move; although with only four (very stiff) extremities, he didn't see how he could possibly travel very far. Fortunately, he couldn't hear any noise and that suggested no humans were about. The room had one window and one door. He heard raindrops splashing on the zinc window sill. He hesitated, unsure whether to head towards the door or the window before finally deciding on the window—from there he could see exactly where he was, although he didn't know what good *that* would do him. He tried to twist around with all his might. He had some strength, but it was evident he didn't know how to channel it, and each movement he made was uncoordinated, aimless, and unrelated to any other. When he'd learned to use his extremities, things would improve considerably, and he would be able to leave with his family in tow. He suddenly realized that he was thinking, and that flash of insight made him wonder if he'd ever thought in his previous incarnation. He was inclined to think he had, but very feebly compared to his present potential.

After numerous attempts he finally managed to hoist his right arm on top of his torso; he thus shifted his weight to the left, making one last effort, twisted his body around, and fell heavily, face down. His family warily beat a retreat; they halted a good long way away, in case he made another sudden movement and squashed them. He felt sorry for them, put his left cheek to the ground, and stayed still. His family moved within millimeters of his eyes. He saw their antennae waving, their jaws set in a rictus of dismay. He was afraid he might lose them. What if they rejected him? As if she'd read his thoughts, his mother caressed his eyelashes with her antennae. Obviously, he thought, she must think I'm the one most like her. He felt very emotional (a tear rolled down his cheek and formed a puddle round the legs of his sister), and, wanting to respond to her caress, he tried to move his right arm, which he lifted but was unable to control; it crashed down, scattering his family, who sought refuge behind a container of liquid softener. His father moved and gingerly stuck his head out. Of course they understood he didn't want to hurt them, that all those dangerous movements he was making were simply the consequence of his lack of expertise in controlling his monstrous body. He confirmed the latter when they approached him again. How small they seemed! Small and (though he was reluctant to accept this) remote, as if their lives were about to fork down irrevocably different paths. He'd have liked to tell them not to leave him, not to go until he could go with them, but he didn't know how. He'd have liked to be able to stroke their antennae without destroying them, but as he'd seen, his clumsy movements brought real danger. He began the journey to the window on his front. Using his extremities, he gradually pulled himself across the room (his family remained vigilant) until he reached the window. But the window was very high up, and he didn't see how he could climb that far. He longed for his previous body, so small, nimble, hard, and full of legs; it would have allowed him to move easily and quickly, and another tear rolled down, now prompted by his sense of powerlessness.

As the minutes passed, he slowly learned how to move his extremities, coordinate them, and apply the requisite strength to each arm. He learned how to move his fingers and gripped the windowsill. Seconds later he finally succeeded in raising his torso. He thought that was a real victory. He was now sitting down, legs crossed, with his left shoulder leaning on the section of wall under the window. His family stared at him from one corner of the room with a mixture of admiration and panic. He finally pulled himself on to his knees, grippcd the sill with his hands, so he wouldn't fall, and looked out of the window. Part of the building on the other side of the street stood out clearly. It was a very long, dark building, with symmetrical windows that broke up the monotony of the façade. It was still raining: big drops of rain that were easy to spot individually and hit the ground separately. He made one last effort and pulled himself up and stood erect. He marveled at being so vertical, yet felt uncomfortable at the same time, even queasy, and had to lean on the wall so as not to fall down: his legs soon went weak, and he gently eased himself down until he was back on his knees. He crawled towards the door. It was ajar. He had to push it to open it wide, and he pushed so energetically (he found it difficult to estimate the effort strictly necessary for each gesture he made) that he slammed it against the wall and it swung back and almost shut. He repeated the movement, less brusquely this time. Once he'd managed to open the door, he went out into the passageway, still on his knees.

Could humans be somewhere in the house? Probably, but (he imagined) if he did find any, they wouldn't hurt him; he looked like them now. The idea fascinated him. He'd no longer have to run away for fear they'd crush him underfoot! It was the first good thing about his transformation. He saw only one drawback: they would want to speak to him, and he wouldn't know how to reply. Once he was in the passage, he pulled himself up again with the help of his arms. He didn't feel so queasy now. He walked along slowly (his legs bore his weight better now) and every step forward he took became easier. There was a door at the end of the passage. He opened it. The bathroom. A toilet, bidet, bathtub, and two washbasins under their respective mirrors. He had never looked at himself before and now saw immediately what he was like: naked, fat, and flabby. From his height in the mirror he deduced he wasn't yet an adult. Was he a child? An adolescent? He was upset to see himself naked; he didn't understand why—nudity had never bothered him before. Was it the misshapen body, the pounds of flesh, the chubby, acne-ridden face? Who was he? What was he all about? He walked through the house, gaining in stability all the time. He opened the door to the bedroom that was next to the bathroom. There were some skates next to the bed. And lots of pennants on the walls. There was also a desk, exercise books, reading books. And a shelf full of comics, a football, and some photos. A photo of himself (he recognized himself straightaway, just like in the bathroom: fat, spotty, and dressed as if for indoor football, in a blue jersey with a white stripe on each sleeve). He found clothes in the cupboard: underpants, a T-shirt, a polo, tracksuit bottoms, socks, and sneakers. He got dressed.

He looked through the spy-hole in the front door. Outside he could see a landing and three more front doors. He went back to the living room, ran his finger along the spines of the few books on the shelves. He caressed a china mug. Turned on the radio. Music blared out, but he couldn't understand the words:

> . . . unforgettable doves,
> unforgettable like the afternoons
> when the rain from the sierra
> stopped us going to Zapoopan . . .

He switched it off. Silence. Sat down on the sofa. Picked up the channel-changer. Turned on the TV. Changed channels; brightened the colors as much as he could, turned the volume all the way up. Turned it all the way down. It was so easy. There was a book open on the sofa. He picked it up, convinced he would understand nothing, but the second he looked at the page, he read almost fluently: "I've moved. I used to live in the Duke Hotel, on the corner of Washington Square. My family has lived there for generations, and when I say generations I mean at least two-hundred or three-hundred generations." He closed the book, and when he'd put it back where he'd found it, he remembered he'd found it open and not shut. He picked it up again, and while he was looking for the page it had been open to, he heard the sound of keys turning in a lock. A man and a woman appeared; *they* were clearly adults. The man said, "Hello." The woman walked over, kissed him on the cheek, looked him up and down, and asked: "How come you've put your pants on backwards?" He looked at his tracksuit bottoms. How was he to know they were back to front? He shrugged his shoulders. "Have you done your homework?" the man asked. Oh, no, not homework! He imagined (as if he could remember) an earlier time, when homework and backward pants didn't exist. "Get on with it then!" It was the woman's turn. Before going to his bedroom and getting on with it, he went into the kitchen, opened the fridge, took out a can of Diet Coke, that he struggled to open (still being clumsy with his hands), and spilled half on the floor. Before they could scold him, he went to the junk room, and as he unhooked the mop, he spotted three beetles huddling against the wall; after freezing for a moment, they tried to escape. He felt disgusted, put his right foot on them, and pressed down until he could feel them squashing.

A Hunger
and Thirst
for Justice

The fact he had been born into an aristocratic family didn't mean Robin Hood couldn't hate social inequality. From his childhood, he'd always felt indignant when he saw how the poor lived in abject poverty while the rich wallowed in luxury. Robin Hood was repelled by a contrast that left the rest of his family unfazed.

He was sure the powers-that-be were always on the side of the wealthy, and he couldn't simply stand by and watch that degrading spectacle, so one day he decided to do something about it. He selected the richest of the rich families in the county. He didn't even need to spy on them to execute the plan he had in mind. He knew them all so well: he was familiar with their every move—where, when, and what they did, when exactly they could be taken by surprise. Then he fixed a day to do the deed. But he had to dress for the occasion. He couldn't wear his usual garb; they'd recognize him. He opted for a black silk mask and a hunting cap, complete with a slender, gray feather from the trunk in the attic that his Uncle Richard had brought him from a visit to the Tyrol. He took his bow, quiver, and arrows and mounted his best steed.

From afar he could see the castle-windows lit up and hear the music pouring out. As he had anticipated, they were throwing a party. Perfect. That way he'd catch them all together, and the pickings from his choice selection of the wealthy and their guests would be rich. He burst into the house, indifferent to the mess his horse's muddy shoes were making on the deep red carpet. The *crème de la crème* of local society was present: not only the hosts (the richest of the rich, the owners of the castle, the main target of his incursion), but also their friends: marquis, counts, and dukes, who were possibly not as rich but in any case were excessively rich when compared to the community as a whole.

It was an exceptional harvest. He stole their tiaras (silver, gold, and jewel encrusted silver), their rings (none was unadorned: all were as thick as the links of a chain), their earrings (some were long and hung down to the shoulder), their keepsakes (one made of platinum), and hair slides (of more varied quality). He put all the money they were carrying in a sack, in a jumble of coins and notes, and ordered the castle-owners (the richest of the county's rich) to open their strongbox and empty it out. He bundled the silver cutlery and candelabra into the same sack and put all the food he found in the pantry into a blue velvet bag. (So many delicious tidbits the needy never got to taste!) Then, still unrecognized by the revelers, he galloped off into the night. The richest of the rich and their aristocratic friends, excited by his feat (that interrupted the monotony of their existences), decided to dispatch lackeys the next morning to take the news to friends who hadn't been with them that night: a masked man had come and had stolen their jewels, valuable possessions, and money. They invited them to an orgy in their castle, so they could tell them the whole story in detail.

Robin Hood galloped through the forest, from west to east, with a clear objective in mind. He had taken two weeks to select the poorest of the poor inhabitants of Sherwood: a family who lived in a wretched timber shack next to an open drain. The poverty-stricken family saw Robin Hood riding up from afar and hid. Whenever anybody went near them, it was always to steal the little they had. Sometimes masked robbers in horizontally striped shirts, sometimes tax collectors in checkered jackets, and sometimes gentlemen in need of fresh meat for a banquet. Robin Hood knocked on their door and asked them to open up: he came in peace. The poor people didn't respond. Robin Hood persisted: "Open up, I bring you what I have robbed from the rich!" They paid no heed. He was forced to smash the door down. The poor people were huddled in a corner of the only room in their hovel (an all-in-one lobby, dining room, kitchen, and bedroom), shaking and begging for mercy. Robin Hood told them they shouldn't be afraid and told them again that he was going to give them what he'd robbed from the rich. "My idea is this," he repeated, "steal from the rich and give to the poor." He repeated the idea several times because they didn't understand him at first. They looked at each other and at him, and were frightened. Robin Hood explained himself, yet again. He was proud of his own distinctive idea of justice. As some would say, "He takes justice into his own hands!" But, take note! He didn't do so to benefit himself but to help others. He robbed the rich (that was clearly a crime: the fact that someone was rich doesn't give anyone *carte blanche* to attack their inalienable right to private ownership, at least not in a market economy), but didn't do so to keep their property for himself, as any common or garden-variety thief would have done, but to hand it on to the needy; he didn't touch a cent. Robbing the rich to give to the poor was an act of generosity that, he was sure, granted him forgiveness in the eyes of God for his premeditated felony. Did the end justify the means? It did as far as Robin Hood was concerned, beyond the shadow of a doubt. That was why he confronted the sheriff, the powers-that-be, and the landowners, whether ecclesiastical or not. Similarly, he always tried to treat women, the poor, and the humble extremely courteously.

But the fruits of his robbery soon vanished. A poor, numerous family, like the one he'd chosen, with a centuries-old hunger in their bellies, rapidly squandered the food, and the money, and sold the candelabra, earrings, and silver cutlery on the black market for a pittance. The poor were still poor, and in no time the rich purchased new candelabra, new silver cutlery, new earrings, and new rings. Perhaps the poor had assuaged their hunger a little, and the rich had lost some money, but the disparity remained huge.

Once again Robin Hood sought out his black silk mask and feathered cap. He rode his steed along winding, labyrinthine paths that cleft the forest and returned to the castle owned by the richest of the rich who, on this occasion, were in the midst of a debutantes' ball. They were astonished. "Not you again?" They didn't find him as exciting as the first time round. One or two even complained: "I hope you don't make a habit of this." Robin Hood took their earrings (emeralds and pearls), tiaras (one was Greek, from Empúrias, handed down from mother to daughter across the centuries), rings (rubies, pure gold, lapis lazuli), bracelets, clasps (one made from ivory that Robin Hood found immensely beautiful), and a pearl necklace. One woman complained because she'd just purchased the earrings Robin Hood stole from her—to replace the ones he'd taken on his first visit. She was particularly annoyed because tracking down an identical pair had been a real pain. She tried to persuade him that her plea for mercy was entirely justified: if he were to steal those, she'd never find another pair: they were the last ones available. Robin Hood was unmoved, snatched them off of her, and put them in the sack with everything else. There were no candelabra. Robin Hood was surprised and asked why. They hadn't had the time to go and buy new ones, the owner of the castle apologized. To compensate, he stole their bed linen, the

Poussin painting, *Bachannal*, that was on the living room wall, and a Richard II chest of drawers. When the sack was full, Robin Hood crossed the forest in an easterly direction, toward the hovel of the poor family; they welcomed him with open arms and tear-filled eyes. "And about time too," said the father, "we were on our last legs."

The next time Robin Hood found the rich even less disposed to welcome him in. People complained while he was filling his sack with money (only one woman, caught napping, was wearing jewels: a silver hair-slide set with two rubies), carpets (three from Persia and one from Turkmenistan), a glass cabinet, and two beds. There was even a duke who tried to resist. Robin Hood kicked him unconscious. The rest of the revelers screamed. Robin Hood spurred on his steed and sped into the forest. The poor family welcomed him with whoops of delight; although, when they saw what he'd brought, one half complained because the booty was less bountiful than on the previous occasions.

In addition to his thirst for justice, Robin Hood had another virtue: perseverance. He repeated his incursions methodically. In the process he stole crockery, pillows, sofas, tables, and armchairs. He stole books, shelves, an umbrella stand, and armor (a whole suit: helmet, visor, chin-guard, gorget, neck and shoulder armor, breastplates, arm-guards, elbow pieces, gauntlets, halberd, thigh-guards, cod-piece, knee-guards, greaves, shoes, round shield and sword). From the wall, he took a Frenchified oblong, four-sided azurite coat-of-arms with a golden tree and two lions propping up its trunk; a gold frame with seven red fleurs-de-lis, arranged in two pairs and a threesome—sealed by a closed helmet and set opposite azure and silver mantling—and, for a crest, a fleur-de-lis pennant coming out of the helmet. He filched the remaining beds, a three-piece suite, and stoves. He dismantled wardrobes, gathered together desks, bureaus, bunk beds, glass cabinets, waste-paper bins, standard lamps, pouffes, children's toys, kitchen sinks, towel-rails, sculleries, bathtubs and sinks, bidets, scales, medicine chests, shower curtains, torches, fire-lighters, stools, linen curtains, bottles (of whisky, cognac, and wine), and fireplaces.

Until one day, a long time afterwards, the rich, in rags, went down on bended knees before Robin Hood and spoke to him, imploring, "Mr. Robin Hood, we don't question your goodness, noble spirit, and legendary generosity. We know you did it for the common good, to bring justice to mankind and compensate for the social inequalities perpetuated by the right to inherit. But you must consider that things aren't what they used to be, that all we have left are these four walls. We have to sleep on the ground, because you even took our beds from us. We have no blankets to keep us warm, no saucepans to heat water and hoodwink our hunger. Mr. Hood, what more do you want from us? There is nothing more to take! We only have these walls, because you've taken even our roofs."

Robin Hood was taken aback. He only needed to take one glance at what used to be a splendid castle not very long ago to see the truth in what they said. Their walls had been stripped and their rooms gutted, and the wealthy of old now slept in the corners, sheltering from the rain that poured in through where the roofs used to be. The rich were rich no longer. It was quite obvious they were poorer than the poor of old who had become richer than they, partly because of the wealth Robin Hood gave them and partly because of the skillful investment policies they'd pursued, thereby multiplying their wealth. But Robin Hood, so generous, obsessive and obstinate, had continued to steal from the rich, who were now, frankly, very poor, to give to the poor, who were, frankly, very rich. His generous attitude had turned the world upside down, to such a point that now (this was his sudden insight) the rich lived in abject poverty and the poor wallowed in conspicuous extravagance and had transformed what was previously a hovel into a complex of mansions, with a swimming pool, sauna, and all the latest paraphernalia. It had been years since the castle hosted its last party; on the other hand, the residential estate where the poor of old lived now celebrated weekly barbecues, if not a bacchanal. How come he'd not noticed before? He looked at the rich, the people he'd seen as exploiters, with a fresh pair of eyes and imagined the financial jamboree being enjoyed by those he'd thought of as poor until not so very long ago. He raged in anger. From his childhood he'd always felt indignant when he saw how the poor lived in abject poverty while the rich wallowed in luxury. He donned his black silk mask, straightened his hunting cap, with the slender, gray feather his Uncle Richard had brought back from the Tyrol. He grasped the reins of his steed, pointed it eastwards, and lashed its back with those very same reins.

3

A Day
Like Any
Other

The compulsive liar has spent an hour on his terrace, soaking up the sun. It's a pleasant feeling after a cold winter, but a moment comes when all that sun makes him feel queasy. He puts a hand over his eyes, gets up from the lounger, goes inside, slips on a shirt and jacket, and walks out into the street. While he's crossing the esplanade, he stares at the abandoned car that's been parked by the football ground for two years and now has neither wheels nor doors. Why the hell don't they move it and turn it into scrap metal? A heron flies low over the cemetery. He turns left and takes the long, sloping road.

He walks past the bar that's halfway down the road; he stops when he's about to leave it well behind. He wonders for a moment whether to go in or not and finally decides he will: he pushes the door open and lets out a general, Good day, to the owner and some customers who are playing dominos. He leans on the bar and orders a beer. The waiter serves him and, inevitably, asks how life's treating him. The liar says, Well, and gulps his beer. His mustache is coated white. A poorly tuned radio is blaring out a melody punctuated by sounds that usually express pain. He watches the dominos game for a while. One of the players asks him if he wants to join in the next round, and he waves a hand to indicate that he doesn't. He turns round, takes another gulp of beer, and gazes at the Russian salad under the glass cover. The golden-brownish hue of the mayonnaise makes him feel like ordering some. The owner sees him looking its way and asks him if he wants some. The liar says he doesn't, because if he eats something now he won't want dinner and his wife will nag. The owner smiles because it's a standard joke: the liar isn't married, he lives alone and always uses his imaginary wife as his excuse. When, for instance, he wants to leave and the others insist he has one for the road, or when they say he should play football with them on Sunday, and he doesn't feel like it. He sometimes adds in children for good measure: a girl who, depending on the day, is between three and seven years old, and a boy who initially didn't exist and is now even older than his sister. The owner washes a glass under the tap and is about to follow their ritual, extending the liar's joke about the would-be wife by asking him whose wife, given he doesn't have one. But before he can open his mouth, the liar asks him loudly—so everyone can hear—if he's seen the circus they're setting up on the esplanade. The owner is now drying the glass. Nobody answers. The liar turns to face the dominos players and continues in the same vein: There are three trailers, one of them huge and cage-like. One of the players raises an eyebrow, looks at him, and says, Of course there are. The liar pretends to be indignant: What does he mean "of course"? Is he implying it's not true? He swears they're setting up a circus on the esplanade. He's seen the letters on the ground; they're made of bulbs that will soon light up on the signboard on the tent: RUSSIAN CIRCUS. The tent, he now adds, is almost erected. There are four trailers. No, five, not four. And six cages: with lions and tigers. And three elephants: big as houses. The dominos players have finished their game and stare at him in astonishment: How can he be trying to make them believe yet another of his lies? However much goodwill they might feel toward him, how could they believe a man who always lies, who lies even when there's no need to lie, when he won't reap any benefit from lying? Their disbelief doesn't waver for a moment or give way to doubt, but, as always happens, the liar speaks so convincingly and so heatedly that, as usual, they don't believe him, but they are fascinated by the passion with which he tells and elaborates his lie. The elephants, for instance, soon become twelve rather than three; the tent is a triple, not single, affair; and the trailers, parked beside it in serried ranks, soon occupy an area the size of a football pitch. As he listens to what he is saying, one of the dominos players (they've finished the game and haven't yet started another) feels his eyes begin to blur. No circus has come to town in thirty years, and he's sure, at the rate things are going, that no circus will ever erect its tent on the esplanade again. None of them misses having the circus (not even the liar, although he'd argue the opposite if need be), and if a circus ever did come, they wouldn't be at all interested: circuses belong to bygone times, and even then people weren't interested. However, their lack of interest doesn't stop them from listening, fascinated by the way he unrolls the canvas sails and erects one tent after another, how he makes the drums roll and multiplies the number of acrobats with such conviction—even though he never thought any of them believed him, let alone that, by virtue of his persistence, he himself would believe his own story. Only one (on the deaf side) asks in an unduly loud voice if anyone wants another game. But nobody answers: someone else has already suggested immediately going to the esplanade. He doesn't need to twist their arms. They now harangue each other, put on their coats and scarves, and are in the street, walking next to the liar, who's describing a pyramid of thirty-six tightrope artistes riding eight unicycles and a horse that can juggle. The last to leave is the owner, who puts on his jacket, pushes out the guy who's on the deaf side, locks the door, and breaks into a run in order to catch the group of men who are hurrying along the road.

Life Is
So Short

The man runs towards the third elevator that has just started to close; he manages to stick his right foot into the small space that's still open, which is enough to make the two sides of the door immediately shoot open. He steps inside and greets the woman who is there already with a "Hello!"; she is very beautiful, with cascading tresses of hair and chestnut colored lips. The man (inhibited by the thought that he'd glimpsed a censorious glint in her eyes, because he'd re-opened the doors and stopped the elevator) stands to one side, looks at the buttons, sees 9 is lit up, takes a step forward, presses 12, that lights up, and goes back to where he was standing. The door closes slowly. He tries not to look at the woman too brazenly. But he can't stop himself from looking at her out of the corner of one eye. Her eyes, chin, legs . . . The door closes, the elevator begins to go up. The numbers light up on the indicator: 1, 2 . . . Piped music plays a sanitized tune. The man looks at his wristwatch. It stopped a while ago. He shakes it, as if shaking will bring it back to life; that used to work with wind up watches, not with the battery kind. It's a slow elevator, and the slowness helps underline the impression of safety suggested by the thick, protective walls. The clean state of the interior also reinforces this impression. A dirty elevator seems abandoned and, hence, unsafe. This one isn't: it is spick and span and new. 5 has already lit up on the indicator and now it will be 6's turn. When 6 lights up, the elevator stops, the doors open, and a bespectacled old man wearing a small hat pokes his head inside.

"Going down?"

The man says they aren't. The old man wrinkles his nose and disappears to the right, index finger at the ready, clearly intending to summon the second elevator, unaware it's out of order and being repaired on the ground floor. The door closes again. For a second, the woman glances at the man, and their eyes meet. He smiles. She averts her gaze. They can see 7 light up on the indicator and then 8. They are midway between the eighth and the ninth floors (8 is still lit up on the indicator and 9 has yet to show) when the elevator stops. The man looks from the woman, to the button panel, to the door ("Here we go again!"). The woman looks at him, the button panel, and the door. The woman is the first to express dismay ("Now what?") and the man the first to try to act as if everything is under control ("Above all, we must not panic."). The woman presses 9, 12, and the ground floor buttons, and when none responds, she asks the man if they should push the button sporting the image of an alarm bell. The man agrees. So they press the alarm button, and the bell immediately rings loud and clear, as if it was on the other side of the elevator walls. Where on earth is it? On the ground floor? In the concierge's office? Is there more than one? From time to time they stop pressing the bell and listen hard, to see if they can hear any noise, someone who's heard them and started the rescue operation or, at least, is nearby and shouting to them reassuringly. But they hear nothing, except for the piped music that churns out song after song, quite oblivious.

A few minutes afterwards the woman introduces herself ("Since it looks as if we're going to have to coexist a while . . ."), the man follows suit and tries to bring a touch of humor by asking if she suffers from claustrophobia. The woman smiles: No, she doesn't. He doesn't either ("We must consider ourselves fortunate. If one of us did, it would be horrible for both.") She's still smiling, and he thinks her smile seems promising. Obviously, trapped inside the elevator as they are, in between floors, in the few minutes they've been stuck there, each has had time to reflect, if only fleetingly, on the so-called urban myths that exist about their situation (two people trapped in an elevator that has come to a halt between two floors), that parallel equally bright ideas about what a man and a woman do on a deserted island, absolutely alone and isolated from the world, though heaven knows for how long. He recognizes that he indeed feels attracted to her, but is *she* attracted to him?

The woman asks if anything important or urgent brought him to the office block this morning. He says it is relatively important ("Work issues.") and remarks how strange it is to be trapped in there (for three quarters of an hour by now) and feel that nothing is, in fact, important any more. She too finds it most striking that the urgent matters bringing them to the building can, all of a sudden, cease to be important because of something quite untoward. An hour ago, she continues, her time was all mapped out and she couldn't have afforded to waste a second. Now, suddenly, she can assume the whole day's been wasted. At the very least, the morning. Will they take much longer to extricate them? The man dares to say she certainly appeared to be in a rush, because when he stuck his foot in between the sides of the sliding door, he thought she seemed peeved. The woman smiles and admits she can't stand people who, when elevator doors start to close, poke their foot in, never thinking that, as far as the individuals inside are concerned (who want to go up or down as quickly as possible, and who in fact have already begun the process one way or the other and are totally within their rights), such a gesture seems extremely inconsiderate. The man is about to say that, at least, putting his foot in the door has had one positive outcome: they have met. But fortunately he nips that banality in the bud. She mentions a Woody Allen film in which an elevator plays a central role. Brian de Palma has one too, starring his wife, what was her name? She is so pretty. He says he once read a novel in which an elevator goes through the roof and flies into the sky.

The elevator, she tells him, is the most important means of transport over the last few decades, even though most people don't think of it as a means of transport. The relationship between elevators and the tall buildings that are being built now provides much food for thought. It's not so much that buildings have had elevators installed because they have grown taller and taller; on the contrary, they have grown taller and taller because elevators have become increasingly efficient and safe. She removes her high-heeled shoes and arranges them in a neat line in the corner, under the button panel. Every now and then, one of them presses the alarm bell for several minutes. When one is tired, the other takes a turn, but in the end they both get fed up and sit on the floor side by side. ("They'll get us out of here soon. They can't leave us here forever." "Perhaps we'll end up eating each other like shipwrecked sailors in order to survive.") The woman thinks it is significant that they are sitting side by side.

For a moment while they are waiting, they lose all notion of time. "Don't look at your watch," says one. It is relatively easy for them to count, second by second, to thirty, and do a half-minute. It's more difficult to count, second by second, to five minutes or half an hour. If they were to count second by second for a few hours, their margin for error would skyrocket.

Later, they fall asleep. They wake up simultaneously ("Did you hear a noise?") in a half embrace, one head on the other's shoulder, their eyes so close that, when one whispers an unintelligible sentence, the other opens his or her mouth and says "What?" and one set of lips draws near the other, although, suddenly, they come to a halt (six millimeters from their objective) because, at that very moment, the elevator moves, accelerates quickly, stops (with a final judder), and reaches the ground floor, where the concierge and one of the repair mechanics are waiting ("You both all right?"). The man and woman look at each other. They should say something, arrange to meet . . . But she thinks that, even though he's staring at her, he's not in a hurry to suggest any such thing, and he reflects that though she's staring at him, she heads straight to the fourth elevator, the one furthest away—not interested, he'd say. Now that their situation in the elevator is all over, is *everything* all over? The man heads out into the street, thinking that he shouldn't have left without fixing a date, or at least exchanging phone numbers. At the precise moment he hits the sidewalk, he wonders why on earth he is walking out if he was supposed to go to the twelfth floor. He half turns round, opens the door into the building, crosses the lobby, avoiding the mechanic and concierge who are observing another mechanic, high up in the ceiling of the new elevator that has broken down, wielding an enormous torch and checking the traction, brake cables, and the guides. The man runs towards the fourth elevator; it has just begun to close, but he manages to stick his right foot into the small space that's still there, thus prompting the two sides of door to slide open immediately.

The Power
of Words

While they set his table, the man waiting at the restaurant bar talks to himself. As a kid he'd heard it said thousands of times: a man who talks to himself is mad. He is now of the opinion that this isn't true. He is quite aware that talking to himself doesn't prevent him from being completely sane. He talks quietly. He whispers sentences, in animated, exciting conversation with another person, or several others, who are all invisible, are all him. He's doing it now, at the bar, and does it driving his car, and at home, and at the office. He talks to himself even when he's with somebody else. Sometimes this somebody hears him whispering and thinks he's said something to him and asks him what he's just said. He says nothing, because in fact he does say nothing (he doesn't even know exactly what he says; rather it's the buzz that interests him, the sonorous effect, the blah-blah-blah, the appearance of a conversation), and whatever he does say he's not saying to the person who's trying to talk to him but to this other invisible person (or persons) with whom he is conducting an on-going conversation. He can't remember when he started talking to himself and would find it difficult to establish the frontier between a before, when he still only talked to other people, and an afterwards. He sometimes thinks that, one way or another, he has always talked to himself; the only thing that has changed is that he's increasingly casual about the whole business and does it quite spontaneously, unthinkingly, quite unaware, never holding himself back. Depending on how you look at it, he sometimes tells himself, these conversations are simply the continuation of the imaginary conversations he pursued when he was a kid, with that friend of his he invented (whose name he can't remember, curiously) and with whom he experienced adventures full of palm trees and lianas every night in bed. The conversations he has with these non-existing others are as interesting as the ones he engages in with real people, when he has no choice. What *does* he talk about when he seems to be addressing his glass? About nothing in particular and about everything under the sun. He might be talking about tennis or philosophies of life. He might be rambling, be aspiring to reach sophisticated levels of argument, or be totally vacuous. This is often the case: he's been debating with himself a good while and realizes that everything he says to this other person is completely vacuous. Then, rather than shut up, he changes the subject.

On the other hand, the man sitting at that restaurant table, surrounded by people deep in animated conversation, says nothing. He's been imperturbably silent for years. Other people's views about his silence are, by now, accepting. They all respect the fact that he silently watches how they reason, argue, and refine shades of meaning which are themselves susceptible to refinement. Precisely because he keeps quiet, they don't know that he thinks what they are discussing is banal, but they assume that must be the case. Generally, they also assume he doesn't have a particular aversion towards them and that his evaluation of their banality isn't at all contemptuous but is, in fact, agnostic. Agnostic in relation to others and himself. He's not against them; he simply passes. He feels he is totally banal and dispensable, and that is precisely why he keeps quiet. He'd find it difficult to judge others for being banal when he himself is guilty of banality. He started to keep quiet the day when, in the midst of a conversation that was drifting into a disquisition on the degree of influence the *fandango* had exercised on the origins of the *huapango*, he suddenly found he didn't know what to do. He knew nothing about the *fandango* or the *huapango*; they were subjects that had never interested him, and consequently, he had absolutely nothing to say. What was he supposed to do, stick his oar in and participate as expected? Invent an opinion on the matter and defend it? Rather than do that, for the first time in his life he preferred to keep quiet. Until that point he had always joined in, even with genuine interest, and forcefully, in all kinds of conversation and arguments. Although the others all looked astonished, he felt he had done no harm by saying nothing. And he didn't find saying nothing at all unpleasant. The others didn't act particularly aggressively towards him. He was used to defending entirely unexpected points of view, and he felt a sense of liberation when he allowed himself the luxury of keeping quiet and not saying a word. He saw how the others kept heatedly debating this or that, and now and again they looked his way, hoping to find he'd had a change of heart and would contribute an opinion. They only needed him to play his part in those ritual nightly conversations. The proof was that he could answer, as a matter of form, with a few predictable words. They found that altogether natural. Because they didn't expect a really genuine or thoughtful response from him: the most formulaic reply sufficed, if it wasn't out of place. His present silence, however, challenged the others' chatter, and this was what upset them, much more than his silence in itself. Finally, a few hours and strange looks later, someone addressed him, asking if he had anything to say. He shook his head almost imperceptibly. The others continued their debate, reckoning that everyone has his day of silence. Nevertheless, he didn't open his mouth in subsequent conversation. From that time on he has said nothing, ever, anywhere. He knows some believe he is being snobbish, that he is putting on airs and being unsociable. He doesn't see it like that. He has absolutely nothing of interest to say; hence he says nothing and listens to the others' heated arguments.

Like, for example, the guy at the other end of the table, who talks fifteen to the dozen, the most talkative of all the people sitting there, the one who won't let the others get a word in edgewise, the one who rushes to speak first, so nobody can beat him to all the clichés available on today's topic of conversation. He has an opinion on everything and wouldn't, for all the tea in China, let himself be caught without a pertinent opinion on any issue whatsoever. He knows (or presumes to know) about economics and art, about stockbreeding and basketball. There isn't a single subject on which he can't express four pertinent ideas that may, sometimes, even scintillate. Given the wide range of topics he is obliged to hold forth on, his four ideas generally have to be transferable, polyvalent and sufficiently ambiguous to address a variety of issues simultaneously. It is not difficult to grasp that, as they have to be capable of adaptation to every possible issue, the insights and subtleties contained within these four ideas are hardly complex. The world is full of conversations where the man who talks fifteen to the dozen has to stick his oar in. He always has to be on the alert for whatever opportunity presents itself to allow him to say whatever comes into his head. Consequently, from time to time he observes the silent man at the other end of the table with a mixture of fascination and pity. How can he endure that almost vegetative existence, watching life pass by and never advancing his opinions? And there is so much to be said! Moreover, he can't help thinking that if he keeps silent it is to make himself seem intriguing, to demonstrate the extent to which he despises everyone around him. On the other hand, he doesn't pity the man he can see seated at the table who is talking to himself, and in fact feels a mixture of envy (because of the self-sufficiency he displays) and respect for what he deems to be a model of perfection.

Literature

He keys in the last sentence with a mixture of excitement and trepidation. It's the first of his novels to end with a death. This is remarkable in itself because dead bodies had been notably absent from his books, a rejection of the facile solutions that so many writers resort to when they don't know how to heighten the drama. Now, for the first time, and driven by the logic of his narrative, he has been forced to change this given and kill his protagonist. He wrenches the page from his typewriter, puts it at the back of all the others, and re-reads the beginning: "That early afternoon, when he was setting the table, the man dropped the salt shaker by chance and some salt fell on the serviettes. He was terrified."

The writer's contract with his publishing house obliges him to write a novel a year. He signed it seventeen years ago, and every January he punctually hands over the new novel to his publisher. He has by now published sixteen novels. He doesn't think writing novels is particularly difficult, and he systematically makes fun of writers who take two years to write one. Sometimes he's happier with some than with others. Sometimes the story flows, he feels passionate; it almost gushes out and is a pleasure to edit. At others the story is contrived;

he writes as if it were a punishment (because, under contract, he must finish, come what may, before the year is up) and struggles to make a few edits. It makes no difference: nobody complains when it's on the feeble side. Insistence on quality is minimal in this country; a situation that is so notorious its inhabitants like to joke about it. His constancy, then, allows him to earn a living—a precarious one, but he doesn't have to get up at 8:00 A.M. His only prayer to this God he doesn't believe in is that he should never have writer's block. That wasn't an option.

His publisher gives him some good news on the day the book is launched: They are going to re-issue his first novel in a new collection, and if he wants, as they have to re-set it, he can re-read it and introduce any changes that he thinks are necessary. He does just that. He has written so many novels that he'd forgotten the precise plot of his first effort and could only remember, rather hazily, some of the characters. He knew it was about a writer who is writing a novel, is quite successful, and that this allows him to publish a second novel the next year and a third the one after that. But when he reads it from one end to the other, he is astonished. The plot and the characters anticipate exact details from his life—events that happened months or years after publication. After sixteen years, he can pinpoint exactly which secondary character the protagonist's wife falls in love with. Because soon after publishing his first novel, he met an identical character, and the woman who fell in love with him was his wife. And the protagonist's struggle against pressure from the world around him was the very same one he faced after his first success.

Intrigued, he reads his other novels one after another, in the order they were written and published. One accurate prediction after another. He recognizes individuals, feelings, sensations, successes, and failures, always written months before the event. He sees his whole life anticipated from book to book. He presages events, situations, women, dramas, and epiphanies. The almighty power of the character in *Green Steppe* anticipates his own power a while after. The anguish of the protagonist in *Pure Soaked Earth* anticipates what he subsequently suffered. And the musician's awareness of his failure in *All the Fire of His Great Sun* was his very own a few months later. He also recognizes actual individuals. The woman in *Colts in the Corral* is Lluïsa, whom he met on the very day of the book's launch. Teresa appears portrayed with almost photographic precision, in *The Spirit*, but when he was writing it, he didn't even know her. He systematically foresaw and wrote things that would happen to him months afterwards.

When he finally comes to his last book, the one he has published a few days ago, he is frightened by the fact that his protagonist dies. He leaves the book on his desk, goes into the kitchen, looks for a can of pre-cooked stew, opens it, pours the contents into a saucepan that he puts into the microwave. He can't recognize any of the characters or events in the book. On the one hand, it's obvious sufficient time hasn't passed for what he's written to turn into reality. On the other, however, the fact he can't recognize anything at all is cause for hope: if it's all about prediction, some of the events should already have happened. That this isn't the case may indicate that this novel is different from the others. Indeed, no law decrees that the norm has to be eternally realized. He thinks all this while setting the table; he is aware of the situation and is going to try to avoid the inevitable.

4

Centripetal
Force

The man has unsuccessfully been trying to leave his apartment since daybreak; whenever he opens the door, the same thing happens: he can't see the landing, only the hallway he's trying to leave at that exact moment. He's tried dozens of times. He tries again: He opens the door to go out, it's dark out there, he takes a couple of steps, touches the wall, gropes for the switch for the light that's next to the elevator. He can't find it. On the contrary, he finds the coat stand, and underneath that, the umbrella stand. So he's back in the hall he's just tried to leave. He stretches a hand out to the hall light switch, finds it, switches it on, and sees that he's standing with his back to his own front door. He turns half around and once again confronts the door. Opens it wide and looks outside. It is very dark, and there's a single patch of light on the floor, the light that is coming precisely from his hallway through the open door, too little light to determine whether beyond his doorstep the landing that's always been there is *still* there, a generously spacious one, as in all old apartment blocks. He could try to leave again, but there would be no point. He's tried repeatedly and unsuccessfully since the early morning. He shuts the door and leans back on it.

He goes into his dining room and looks into the street. Several people are walking up and even more are walking down it. He tries not to get stressed. He must get out one way or another. He picks up his phone, dials a girlfriend's number. It's a girl he's not known very long, and he hasn't yet managed to be intimate with her, which he regrets. Why not? Is it because he's shy? Because he's never had the right opportunity? He thinks that it's perhaps because he's not reached that degree of intimacy with her that he's decided to ask her this favor: She should come to his place immediately. The friend asks why. He adopts an extremely somber tone of voice, and without saying exactly what's wrong (he doesn't tell her because she won't believe him or will think he's mad and won't come), he tells her he is caught in a most unusual situation (not a serious one, but a most unusual one), so unusual that if he tells her on the phone she won't believe him or will think he's gone mad; he needs her help. She says nothing for a few seconds and finally says she will drop by at three, after work.

The man spends the next couple of hours staring at the door and smoking non-stop, until he's filled a vase with butts. In effect, his friend arrives when it's three minutes to three. He briefly tells her what the situation is, as clearly as he can, and before she can react in shock, he tells her what they are going to do: "This is what we are going to do: We will leave the apartment together. If I leave by myself, I will never reach the landing. I always find myself back in my hallway and not on the landing."

She asks, "Why do you think things will be any different if I'm with you?"

He doesn't reply, grabs her wrist, they walk towards the door, he takes a deep breath, turns the handle, opens the door, and they go out; in effect, they reach the landing as he'd predicted. He gives a sigh of relief. She looks at him, taken aback. He presses the button for the elevator. She says there's no point because the elevator is out of order: she'd had to walk up. They walk downstairs. On the ground floor there's a notice on the elevator-door: OUT OF ORDER.

They go for a stroll, look at the shop windows and the colored lights—shaped into stars, little birds, and bells—that decorate the street. She buys two presents for Twelfth Night. A truck and a cement-mixing truck, huge, plastic toys, for her nephews. With those presents for company, they dine out, drink tea in a café until she looks at her watch and says it's time she was going. He takes her right hand in his left.

"Come home with me," he suggests, "don't abandon me. If you do, it will happen again."

The woman laughs and acknowledges nobody's ever used this line on her before, but it's not ingenious enough to persuade her to spend the night in his apartment. They've often talked about doing it. She knows he wants to sleep with her, but for the moment she's happy the way things are. She understands he's frustrated: she knows men can't usually accept the possibility of a straightforward friendship with a woman without sex. He finds her little homily rather tiresome, is annoyed and decides that in fact it would be better if she did clear off. They kiss each other on the cheek; she disappears down into the subway. The man walks on along the street. He can't be bothered (he's not afraid, just can't be bothered) to go home because he knows the minute he's back inside he won't be able to leave. So he decides there's no point rushing back. There's a cocktail bar nearby that he particularly likes, with a wooden floor and ceiling and glass cabinets full of bottles mounted on every wall. He heads there. In the distance he can see the elongated light over the gold nameplate. He pushes the thick, heavy door open, pulls aside the red velvet curtain, and, hey presto!, he's back in his hallway. He turns half around and opens the door again: every step he takes to leave is a step that takes him inside. He turns half around again, opens the door again, leaves again, and comes back in again. He's back inside now.

He decides to try the window. He pulls up a stool, stands on it, opens the window, pulls himself up, and climbs out. It's a narrow sill. The cars look tiny down in the street. In effect, he's managed to leave his apartment through the window and is now precariously balanced. It's cold. He stands there for a time weighing up his next step. It's not that he needs to do anything special. It's fine outside. If there weren't such a wind, it would be even better: being outside means that at least he's gotten out. So he's not simply standing still, he walks slowly along the ledge, his back to the wall, looking out into the void until he's level with the window of the next-door apartment. Inside, his neighbor is helping her son do his homework. Watching these scenes of daily life through windows always makes him feel sentimental. When he walks down the street, he's always on the look-out for an interior in a low-level apartment. A light in a dining room ceiling, two heads around a table, a chunk of shelving, a painting, and someone sitting in an armchair. He doesn't even consider the possibility of knocking on his neighbor's window. He knows that if he does, the shocked, surprised woman will scream, even though she'll recognize him as soon as she opens the window. Naturally, she'd let him in; she couldn't do otherwise, she knows he is her neighbor and must have a very good reason for being on her windowsill. Besides, she is a gossip and wouldn't want to fritter away such a splendid opportunity. But what good would it do? If she doesn't accompany him, once he finally decides to leave his neighbor's flat, he'll only have to walk out of the door and he'll return to his own place without even crossing the landing. He'll only have to open her door to open his and be back to square one. He decides to walk back. He retraces his steps along the ledge, as slowly as he'd come. He's soon close to his window. He's about to twist around and climb back in when he notices a small group of tiny people looking up at him and pointing. He's alarmed. If they're looking at him and pointing like that, it can only mean one thing: they think he wants to commit suicide! Or that he's trying to break into an apartment and steal something. It's a reasonable assumption. Why else would anyone want to walk along that ledge? To steal or to commit suicide. Or take photos. He could be a detective trying to take photos of his client's husband, catch him in the act with a lover. He's been watching them for quite a while. He finds it amusing. More and more people are looking up at him. He's excited to think they think he wants to commit suicide or steal. The traffic soon snarls up. Cars honk their horns, the municipal police arrive, look up at him for a moment, and then blow their whistles and try to restore order. The crowd gets bigger. Soon after, the fire-fighters arrive, siren wailing and revolving light flashing. Seven men get out of their truck. The seven spread out a safety blanket, to give him a safe landing. The man gets even more alarmed (they really *do* think he's going to commit suicide!), he turns round abruptly, pulls himself up, climbs through the window, and is back inside his apartment. He closes the window and takes a deep breath. He looks around and back down into the street. The crowd is still there. He pours himself a glass of water. Sits on his sofa. Sweats. Switches on the TV.

A few minutes later, someone knocks on his door. He gets up and opens the door. Two firefighters stand there: one is extremely fat, making the other one seem comparatively thin, though he's not. They are out of breath. The extremely fat one wipes the sweat from his forehead with a handkerchief, folds it, still breathless, and makes a declaration, as if scolding the tenant: "The elevator's out of order."

The other firefighter takes a step towards him.

"Good evening. Number two on the eighth?" The man nods. "We

have to write a report justifying why we came out. A moment ago a man was near your window, about to jump. Who was it?"

"No, he wasn't going to jump. Let me explain."

Now that the firefighters are here, there is a landing. Is it always like that? If there is someone with him, the landing is there; if he's alone, the landing disappears and he finds his hallway in its stead. His neighbor's door is on the other side of the landing (she's straightening some paintings that are hanging in her hall), it's open a few inches so she can see and hear better. The man invites the firefighters inside, and as he closes his door, he sees his neighbor close hers too. What would happen now, if he tried to leave with the firemen inside? Would he simply come back in or would he find the landing there? To check that out, he apologizes, leaves the firemen in his living room, goes into his hall, opens the door, and as he leaves, comes back into his hallway and shuts the door with a click. But the firefighters aren't in his new hallway. He pokes his head into his dining room: they're not there either. He opens his cocktail bar and pours himself a glass; sits down and watches TV once again.

Twenty minutes later, more knocks at the door. Three more firefighters.

"Good evening. Sorry to bother you. Two colleagues of ours came up to this apartment a while ago to fill out a report and haven't come back down."

"They left some time ago."

"We were waiting downstairs, and we've not seen them." The firefighter with the oversize mustache, who's talking, opens a folder, so he too can fill in a report.

The man invites them in and sees that his neighbor's door is half open. As they walk in, the firefighters take their helmets off. Did the last two do that? He hadn't noticed. The man with the really oversize mustache asks if two firefighters had come to see him. The man nods. He asks him to describe them. The man can't. He hardly looked at them.

"It's a routine question. We need to find out whether the physical description of the individuals who visited you matches our colleagues."

Through his half-open door, the man can see his neighbor is still looking at him from hers, while she pretends to clean the gold-colored spyglass. He waves, indicating she shouldn't shut her door. He speaks to the firefighters, "Excuse me for a moment. I'll be back right away."

He leaves his apartment, gently closes the door, and crosses the landing, with the protection (he intuits) of his neighbor preventing it from transforming into his hallway. The neighbor opens her door. He asks her to let him check something. She invites him in. He goes in. Would she let him climb out of her window for a moment? His neighbor is thrilled to bits and says he can do whatever he likes.

"I can see you've got an apartment full of firefighters," she says while bringing him a three-rung ladder. His neighbor's son immediately stops doing his homework, chews his pencil, and watches them. The man smiles, nods, and climbs out of the window. Keeping close to the wall, he walks slowly along the ledge, as far as the window to his apartment. Down in the street, the crowd is pointing at him again. Near his window, he strains his neck, looks inside, and sees the firefighters holding their helmets. Looking at each other and now and then at the door to see if he's coming back. The crowd in the street had shrunk since his last sally, but it was on the increase again. His neighbor puts her head out of the window. The man walks back slowly.

"Everything's in order."

He pulls himself up. He jumps in, thanks the woman, and they walk towards the hallway. On the landing (here's confirmation: whenever he is with someone, the landing never turns into a hall), he thanks her again, and before closing her door, rather than entering his apartment, he runs downstairs. He reaches the ground floor and goes into the street. A cold wind is blowing and sweeping up sheets of newspapers that fly over the ground until they catch on benches, dumpsters, and the legs of passers-by. He joins the crowd looking up at his apartment.

Half an hour later, the firefighters who went up still haven't come down. One of the two firefighters who stayed in the truck goes up to look for them. The minutes tick by. The flashing light revolves silently on top of their truck. The firefighter, who is now by himself, looks tired. He'd like to be home. Today, there are greens and fish in breadcrumbs for supper. He'd wear his slippers and maroon jersey, and after dinner he and his wife would argue about what to do to relax. Ten minutes later, the three firefighters who went up to get the first two appear in the front entrance to the block, together with the last firefighter to go up. No sign, however, of the first two. Before they reach the truck, the man discreetly moves away in case they recognize him, feeling a guilt he finds altogether unjustified.

•

The extremely fat firefighter closes the book, pants, and puts the book on the coffee table in front of the sofa and plants his feet there too. The comparatively thin firefighter re-arranges the flowers in a vase on the cocktail bar. He moves two steps away, scrutinizes them, and walks back to re-arrange them yet again.

"This guy's not coming. I think we should go."

"There's no rush. We can at least take a break. I'd rather be here than go back to the station and have to go out on another job. Get me another whisky."

"It will be obvious if we drink anymore."

"So what? He must have disappeared three quarters of an hour ago. The least he can do is offer us a whisky. I'll get more ice from the kitchen."

The extremely fat firefighter gets up and goes into the kitchen.

"We really should be going down, I don't give a fuck where he's gone," says the thin man. "Let's do the report and get downstairs."

"The longer we wait, the more likely they'll have repaired the elevator. This is an eighth floor plus the mezzanine." The fat man comes in from the kitchen with two glasses full of ice. The thin man is about to suggest they should definitely go down, when he looks through the window and sees their truck start up and begin to move off.

"They're leaving!"

The fat man runs to the window. They both watch the truck drive downhill, its flashing light revolving non-stop. The two firemen grab their helmets in a rush and leave the flat. They press the button to the elevator, just in case they've repaired it in the meantime. They see that's not the case and head down the stairs.

When they've been going down five minutes, the comparatively thin man stares at the sign on the wall: they've only reached the sixth floor. They stop. It can't be true. They've been going down for such a long time: they should have reached the ground floor ages ago. They've walked down fourteen or fifteen floors, how can they still be on the sixth? They go down one more. The sign says FIFTH. They go down another. But, after the fifth, the floors have no signs. They keep walking down: one, two, three, four more floors. No signs. That's to say: there's a mark where a sign used to be, a rectangle that's lighter than the rest of the wall and the holes where screws must have secured the sign. On the next floor, there is another sign: FOURTH. The floor beneath doesn't have one. The next one doesn't either. Nor the next one. The next one has a sign. The fourth again.

They rest for a moment. The extremely fat man suggests knocking on a door and asking permission to call the station. The comparatively thin man points theatrically at the signs, as if to suggest that all their effort is in vain. But the other man doesn't understand his gesture.

There are two doors on each landing. They put their ears to the nearest door. The one with a two at the top. Number two on the fourth. But they can't hear anything. They run to number one on the fourth. They can hear a television. They look at each other. They don't need to say a word; they both think it's ridiculous for two firemen to be knocking on a door to ask permission to call up the station to get someone to fetch them. They go down another floor. It's the fourth again. They put their ears to the nearest door. In number two on the fourth they can hear several people laughing. A family reunion? A party? At number one on the fourth they can hear the clacking of a typewriter. Who on earth can be typing in this day and age? They go down another floor. It's a landing without a sign. They hear a couple arguing behind the door to number two. The later it gets, the more disheartened the firefighters feel. The truck shouldn't have gone without them. When they get to the station, what excuse will they have for abandoning them? Did they decide to leave because they were taking their time? The sound of someone playing a piano reaches them from a distant apartment. They both imagine it's a woman. She's playing a cheerful tune—badly. La, la, la, do, mi, mi, re, do, B flat, re, do, do, do, do . . . They try in vain to remember the tune's name.

The extremely fat firefighter goes down the stairs, followed by the comparatively thin one. They've decided to knock at a door—the pianist's. They prick their ears up, trying to discover which flat the piano music is coming from. They can hear it increasingly clearly. They finally reach the door through which the music is coming. Not only can they hear it very clearly: some notes are escaping under the door.

The extremely fat firefighter looks at the thin one, who nods and knocks. The piano continues to tinkle away. The firefighter knocks again, more insistently. The piano goes quiet. Can they hear footsteps? They glue their ears to the door. If the piano has gone silent it's because they've been heard. But nobody comes to open up. They knock again. Suddenly, the door opens. A woman's head appears in the gap created by the security chain and gives them the once over, from helmets to boots. Perhaps she is the pianist? Both had imagined her being much younger. The firefighters greet her and say they need to call the station, to tell them to come and pick them up. The woman gives them the once over again, this time from boots to helmets. They feel absurd. The woman closes the door for a second, removes the security chain, opens it wide, and invites them in. They go in. The woman shuts the door and points to her telephone. The thinner firefighter picks up the receiver, puts it to his ear, and dials.

"The line's busy," the thinner firefighter tells the fatter firefighter and the pianist as well. It's obvious she is in fact the pianist: an enormous piano occupies almost the whole room. "How can the fire-station line be busy?"

The pianist gives them a look of irritation, hugging herself and rubbing her arms together against the cold. The thin firefighter says: "If I told you what's happened, you wouldn't believe me."

The fat firefighter suspects the thin firefighter has dialed the wrong number. He takes the receiver and dials. In effect, the line is busy. He hangs up. He looks at the other firefighter. The pianist looks at them, alternately, from one to the other. Suddenly they hear a scream on the stairs.

The scream is repeated. They hear a door open, another scream, louder and clearer now, and several doors open. The pianist goes to her door and opens it. On the landing above, a neighbor, in a padded quilt dressing gown, is saying haltingly, between sobs, that she's just found her husband dead in the hall. Someone forced their door open and killed him.

The pianist turns around and looks questioningly at the firefighters. Before she has time to ask, they both shake their heads and say: "Nothing to do with us."

The pianist opens her mouth wide (a huge mouth, no lipstick, full of teeth and very visible tonsils) and screams. The neighbors peer over into the stairwell. Hundreds of them walk down at once and surround the suspicious firefighters, who defend themselves, repeating time after time that it had nothing to do with them.

"How shameful for the firefighting force!" says the neighbor who has just called the police. In a matter of seconds they hear the wail of sirens and, soon afterwards, cursing the elevator that's still out of order, two policemen appear, handcuff the firemen, and take them downstairs to the ground floor, out in the street, to the police van. Apart from their understandable annoyance at being mistaken for murderers (wrongly of the opinion that their innocence will be proven), they feel relieved to reach the ground floor.

•

The neighbor who was wearing the padded quilt dressing gown is now wearing a black dress and sitting in front of the coffin that is home to what's left of her husband. From time to time she puts a handkerchief to her eyes and wipes a tear away. Her relatives keep her company: the brother-in-law (her husband's brother), two sisters, her son and his fiancée. Not very far away are the neighbors, among whom the pianist enjoys pride of place; she thinks she has a certain right to the privilege, to a kind of superiority over the other neighbors and even over some relatives, especially the ones who are very distantly related—the firefighters were arrested in *her* house. Nonetheless, reasonably enough, the widow is the center of attention and is hugged methodically by everyone present.

When the funeral parlor staff arrives, everyone standing in the circle moves back towards the walls and creates a space around the coffin. When the staff closes the coffin, the widow bursts into a more intense bout of crying: she will never see her husband again, dead or alive. Her son gives her a hug, the funeral parlor staff carry the coffin on their shoulders as her sobbing reaches a crescendo. As the coffin exits the apartment via the door, the widow's sobs reach an even higher pitch. They are all on the stairs now. One of the widow's sisters locks the door and puts the key in her purse. The parlor staff climbs the stairs and slowly starts to bring the coffin down. There are lots of steps, and ensuring they don't drop the coffin is a long, annoying process. Finally, however, they reach the ground floor, open the front door, and walk out. There is a strong, cool breeze. The funeral car is waiting in front of the door, loaded down with wreaths. There are so many that they've had to leave some on the ground—it's impossible to fit them all in without them sticking out of the car, which is against the law. The staff makes one last effort and lifts the coffin inside. The funeral parlor staff dusts their jackets and gets into the car. The relatives divide themselves between the other two, incredibly immaculate cars. The pianist gets into the third car. She is the only person allowed in who isn't a relative; she is truly very proud and watches the rest of the neighbors who remain by the front door, smiling half contemptuously. Some of the women are carrying handkerchiefs and wipe tears and snot away.

They have to drive across the city to reach the highway that will take them to the cemetery. They proceed in a caravan: the first is the funeral car. The other two drive behind in a strict single file. They scrupulously respect the traffic lights and drive very slowly. They take the main road leading to the avenue leading to the highway. There is a lot of traffic, and inevitably, some passengers in the cars overtaking them turn round and gawk. If they are children, their mouths are wide open with fear. It's the first time many of them have seen a car carrying dead people, and they look at the coffin with terror: there's a dead man in there. They finally reach the avenue. The traffic is flowing well now, and the further they drive, the fewer cars they meet. They drive like that for a few minutes until construction suddenly forces them to take a detour. The driver of the funeral car follows the signs, indicating the route of the detour, until gradually there are fewer and fewer signs and the driver has to use his intuition. He decisively takes a turn but finds it's a dead end. He should back out, but the two cars behind him are jammed too close together and he can't. He gets out of the car and asks them to back out, so they can take one of the side roads they've just left and try to get back to the avenue that should take them to the highway, or at least, to the signs. They back up: first the last car, then the second, and finally the funeral car, which accelerates ostentatiously as soon as it's out the bottleneck; this has a negative impact both on the relatives and the pianist. The other two cars, nonetheless, follow on, screeching their tires. They are in an area of the city that's full of shops. There are large industrial parks and (huge) parked trucks. The roads have names unknown to most citizens, them included.

The absence of traffic isn't helpful. On the contrary: if there were traffic, if people were driving along these roads, they could ask someone how to get out of their impasse. They are suddenly forced to turn right and come to a beach that runs parallel to a road. It would make reasonable sense to head left, but when the driver of the funeral car indicates which way he intends to turn, the driver behind honks his horn. He lowers his window and says it's a dead end. They should go right or back the way they came. Although it's in the wrong direction, it is the *only* way to return to the signs. The driver of the funeral car acknowledges that he doesn't know where they are, but deduces that as the metropolitan cemetery is more or less to the north, beyond the first ring of suburbs, they should head northwards along the road: that is, to the left. The few occupants who by this stage haven't gotten out to voice their opinions finally do get out, slamming their doors. The son, the son's fiancée, the brother-in-law, the father, the father-in-law, the mother-in-law, and the pianist have very clear ideas about what to do, even though they're at odds with each other. The widow starts crying again. Finally they decide to take heed of the suggestion made by the driver of the funeral car, simply because they think he's an expert: of the three drivers he is the only one who drives professionally. They return to their cars. They drive off. They head left along the road that runs parallel to the beach. They carry on for a mile or so, until the road runs out in front of a swimming club. The only asphalted exit is to the left, a road even narrower than the one they've just negotiated. They take it. That narrow road soon joins four other equally narrow roads, where there are a few homes. They are simply styled, century-old houses with a ground floor and an upstairs with a balcony and green wooden shutters. All the houses are painted white. The doors on the ground floor are made of glass and wood. They can see people inside: a man watching TV, a girl studying, a man repairing a radio, and a girl at a sewing machine. Some children are playing ball in the street. The driver of the funeral car stops, gets out, and speaks to the women sitting and sewing on chairs outside the door to their house. He asks them how to get off of these side roads and on to the highway. They raise their arms and point their index fingers to the road they've just driven up. The driver says that is precisely where they've come from and that they hadn't been able to find a way off those roads. The deceased's relatives get out of their cars once again. The deceased's son suggests they drive back across the city, go south, along the other highway, the ring road around the whole city, to get to the north, to the small town where the cemetery is. The deceased's brother doesn't agree. They are north of the city. It is ridiculous to drive back across, simply to drive all the way around to where they are now. What they should do is not get into a panic and look for the street that leads to the highway. It must be very close to where they are now: One road or another is bound to lead there. The driver gets back into the funeral car, the others follow suit, drive to the next road, turn left along it, and the next one also to the left, trying to find the wider road that ran out by the swimming club and the beach. But there seems to be no way to get there, and they suddenly find themselves in a rectangular square. It is a square that bears the name of a general from a couple of centuries ago; planted in its center is a tall tree with a gnarled trunk, where two kids are trying to make the other fall off and where there's no other road apart from the one they have just driven along.

5

Strategies

A S soon as the examiner opens the door, the distinctly pale-skinned candidate slips through the crowd of other candidates who are clogging up the doorway. He walks with a spring in his step and takes the first empty chair he finds. The desks are made of light green formica with wooden sides. The tops are covered in pen-ink graffiti and scored by knives; two of the etched phrases are obscene. The din (made by the grating of desks and chairs and the chitchat) increases as the candidates walk in; the examiner asks them to please (it is a drawn-out, imperious "please") sit down without making a sound. The candidates fleetingly pay him some attention; the noise dips for a few seconds, but soon returns to its previous intense level. The examiner turns his back on them: he erases the sentences that were left from the class before from the blackboard and turns around (the noise dips again), and when they are all seated, he walks down from the dais, goes over to the door, shuts it, wipes off the chalk-dust from his hands (a gesture that silences the last whisperers), and calls out two surnames. Two candidates get up from their desks and walk over to him. He gives each of them a pile of stapled sets of paper, which they begin to distribute. As they proceed to put a set on each desk, the pupils strain their eyes trying to read the questions (they are in very small print), but nobody attempts to pull the set of papers towards him or glance deviously at the top sheet. They don't touch anything until they're all given out and the examiner says that they can start. Almost fifty sets of paper rustle in unison around the room. The distinctly pale-skinned candidate takes a deep breath, pulls his set across his desktop so they're right in front of him, and calmly starts to read. He has spent the weekend cramming, and now that the examination has finally begun, he feels a mixture of exhaustion and disinterest. He's spent weeks preparing for this exam, which will determine whether he can progress or not. Years ago he'd have said it was a crucial exam, but over time he has learned that all exams are crucial, to the point that an exam that wasn't crucial wouldn't seem authentic. He has just read the five questions and is feeling relaxed. He knows four of the answers perfectly. Consequently, he can already conclude that he has passed, at the very least. He suddenly realizes he's been tapping on his desktop for quite some time: *ratatatat, ratatatat, ratatatat.* He glances at the other candidates and sees how stressed they all seem. Most are writing in a rush, as if they were going to run out of time, filling one sheet after another, their faces blank. Two are thinking really intensely. That's obvious because they're frowning and staring at the ceiling; what's more, one of them is chewing the end of his ballpoint. Another has lowered his head in order to drop out of the examiner's field of vision and say something to the boy in the next desk: he moves his lips, slowly vocalizing a word, but the student can't hear; he responds by putting his bottom lip over his top lip and shrugging his shoulders. The whisperer silently repeats the word time and again. They carry on like that until the examiner begins to walk up and down the aisles between the three rows of desks. The one stooping down straightens his back, reacting over-seriously and suspiciously. As if he too might be caught in the act, the distinctly pale-skinned candidate also straightens and finally decides to get started. He takes the top off his pen and writes his name. He begins to answer the first question, in clear, even writing, one word flowing after another, in straight, compact lines. When he's finished the first, he starts on the second. But after writing a few lines he feels faint again and stops writing. He is tired. The last few days of intense studying can't have tired him that much; perhaps he's exhausted by the succession of exams he's had to face, year after year, ever since he was a child . . . If only he could see an end to it all . . . But after this exam there will be another and then another. He knows that the preparation requires an effort, that one never knows enough, that one can never properly show how much one knows, whether it's enough or not. However, this knowledge doesn't stop him from wondering whether there will ever be a final exam. He starts to write again, reluctantly. He knows he will pass, as he always does. Everyone always does. Not because the examiners are generous. They are harsh; nevertheless, he hasn't known (and nobody he has known has *ever* known) anyone to fail. Everyone passes, always: because everyone revises conscientiously. The fact everyone has always passed means that the panicking over possible failure is curious, at the very least. Has anyone ever failed? And what's the point of sitting for the exams, if everyone always passes? Because if exams didn't exist, people would stop revising as carefully as they currently do?

The question he's been considering over the last few exams buzzes around his head again: What if he decided to fail on purpose? He's increasingly sure that nothing really serious would happen. If he passed yet again, tomorrow he'd simply start the routine all over again: store away the books he's just studied, open up a new set, and memorize thousands of pages. The walls of his house are covered in books. At first he put them on shelves. Then he ran out of walls and began to pile them up on tables, under his bed, on top of his bed.

Now there were books everywhere. It would be a mistake to get rid of the oldest to make space for new ones, because the new exams often referred to explanations you could only find in books you had studied years earlier as a child preparing for the first exams. Four or five exams ago he realized that he couldn't remember anything about his first exam; the first exam he remembers taking only took place one or two years ago.

Why continue sitting for exams? In fact, what use are they or will they ever be? Wouldn't it be best to give them up now? Just as he can't remember his first exams, he's also forgotten their ultimate goal, beyond turning yourself into a short-lived examiner. He knows that the examiners (who have overcome the hurdle of the exams he's now facing) also sit for exams, but doesn't know why. In order to turn into an (also short-lived?) examiner of examiners? He's not even sure he'll know if he becomes an examiner. Just as he didn't know, when he started as a child, that the first objective (the one he thinks he's on the brink of now) is to become an examiner. He began, he thinks he can recall, because his parents (like absolutely all parents) wanted him to study. But his parents died years ago in a biplane accident, one afternoon when he was sitting for an exam. He tries to recompose the fragments of his childhood and adolescence that he remembers. Has anything he studied ever interested him?

He's bored by the idea he might pass yet again. He's been taking exams and passing without fail for years. Why does he need to show the examiner that he can answer four out of five questions? And how many exams has the examiner had to pass to become one? The very fact there are examiners must prove that there is a final exam. However, can that really be true? Perhaps things are rather more complicated (or more straightforward) than he imagines? Is he close to that final exam, or are there still years to go? And the only way he can challenge his string of passes is, in his opinion, by failing. During the last few exams he's had a strong suspicion that his fellow candidates have or have had the idea that's been buzzing around his head of late: give the wrong answers. He can't possibly be the only one who finds passing one exam after another (eternally) to be quite stupid. Initially his pulse races, but soon he grows in confidence: He answers the questions one by one, in clear, even writing, one word flowing after the other, in straight, compact lines—incorrectly, on purpose. When he finishes, he will get up from his desk, hand his papers to the examiner, and (this is what he's thinking to himself) will fail.

- 2 -

Irrespective of the time he finally gets to bed, on the eve of election day the candidate always sets at least one alarm clock, and two or three if he is very tired or is afraid his usual alarm clock will let him down at the decisive moment. The candidate must be sure he will wake up early enough, although the electoral campaign has in fact finished and theoretically he can allow himself to rest, after weeks of going from one meeting to another and sleeping only two or three hours a night. He must get up early because he knows that on the final straight there are few things that make a worse impact than the candidate who gets to the polling place late, looking sleepy-eyed and unkempt. A candidate who places his vote at noon is a thoughtless fellow that the electorate will dub a slacker: the day his immediate future is at stake, as is, presumably, the city's, his head seems stuck to his pillow. The thinking behind that is clear enough: if he lets laziness rule when he isn't mayor, what will he be like when he is?

It wouldn't matter if his lethargy showed itself afterwards: tonight or tomorrow, once election day is over and done with. But the reports showing the candidates casting their votes will be on the midday television news. And midday is still hours away from when the election stations close, and that makes these reports the last act in the election campaign, although that officially isn't the case. The law rules that the campaign must finish at midnight on the day before the election. However, many potential voters (the people who always leave everything to the last minute, the ones who get to the cinema after the film has started) will see the reports at midday, and the way a candidate comports himself when he votes may in the end make him decide to get up from his sofa and go vote. And even (and this is what's crucial as far as he is concerned) vote for *him*. That's why his attitude at the polling place is so critical, as are the exchanges with the members of the electoral table, his vote, and his subsequent appearance back on the street. A serious, thoughtful expression may have a positive impact on the don't-knows who believe that this candidate has been too lighthearted or arrogant during the campaign. Though others might conclude that this sudden seriousness reflects fear of possible failure, a conclusion that would persuade them not to vote for him. Conversely, a frivolous, facetious attitude, that might appear positive to those who felt he was too distant during the campaign, could be counter-productive if it was interpreted as presumptuous, that he thought victory was already in the bag. It would be unseemly to whistle your way into the voting booth. Bad vibes if you cry and bad if you laugh: and equally bad if you don't cry or laugh.

To compensate for this *via crucis* to the town hall, the candidate has the ultimate advantage: at least theoretically, he is the citizen who should be in the least doubt when it comes to placing his vote. Even family and collaborators could (out of conjugal boredom, envy, or internal intrigue) vote for someone else: to fuck him up or, in their heart of hearts, to feel like schoolboy hooligans once again. But he wasn't allowed any doubts. It's an unwritten law. The possibility of puncturing that particular bubble has indeed been buzzing around the candidate's brain for some time on the way to the polling place, and when he gets out of his car, smiles into the flashes of the photographers, enters the voting hall, and walks through the crowd of voters. And what if he didn't vote for himself? They say that any candidate who is really honest and believes in the program he is putting forward is duty-bound to vote for himself. If he reflects on this dispassionately, however, isn't this vote for oneself, to a certain extent, a kind of spell, a propitiatory magical ritual? He recalls the first time he was able to vote (long before he became a professional politician), the overwhelming emotion, the doubts about whom to vote for and whom not to, his exhaustive scrutiny of the election programs of each of the candidates, his leap of faith. He takes a voting slip for each party, enters the booth, and closes the curtain. The journalists smile and think it's one big joke. He doesn't need to pick up a slip for each party and hide in the booth to decide his vote. Everyone knows whom he is going to vote for, and he doesn't need to keep any secrets.

Alone in the booth, the candidate reviews the slips and thinks that maybe one could formulate the proposition in the opposite way: that a candidate who is so confident of his honesty and the value of his program has no need, at any stage, to be in thrall to superstition. On the contrary: confidence in himself and the power of his arguments should allow him to make a gift of his vote, to present it to his rival—his own arguments are so clearly right they are bound to win over the hearts and minds of the majority, who will ever cast their votes for his opponent? Too bad then if victory is finally decided by his wretched vote. He seals the envelope, opens the curtain, exits the voting booth, smiling broadly and flourishing the envelope containing his vote. In the history of humanity has there ever been another candidate who (as a result of a sudden attack of sincerity, or of schizophrenia), under the protection of the sealed envelope, has voted for his rival?

The curtain rises. The stage set is a dining room. The walls are covered in blue and green flowery paper. In the center, a large redwood table, on the top of which are a vase of flowers and a heap of musical scores (that the theater-goers in the stalls simply see as a heap of paper). On the right, a sideboard; on the left, a fireplace with a plastic log and fake flames. Above the fireplace, a painting of an ugly woman wearing a tiara. The actor strides confidently in and walks towards the table, but he stops halfway. He clicks his tongue and turns around, stops and clicks his tongue again, walks back towards the table. This is his way of trying to communicate a sense of bewilderment, indecision, and grave concern. He places his right hand on the table and, finally, after waiting for the necessary seconds to pass, launches into his monologue. He speaks unhurriedly, in a clear, deadpan tone, and at a brisk tempo. It is a long monologue; the author wrote it so that the character can reflect on the harshness of existence, the dubious life he has led to that point, and his bitterness at the realization of having made so many mistakes and wasted so much time. All these reflections mean that every day the actor inevitably (as he continually repeats his lines) thinks that it is indeed a bitter pill to acknowledge one's mistakes, and (while he lists those his character has made) he reviews in parallel those he himself has made throughout his life, the last being precisely his agreeing to take on this role in a play he finds increasingly awful. Even though he's an experienced actor, he doesn't find it easy to simultaneously maintain the flow of words in his speech and allow his own thoughts to wander. In fact, he ought to concentrate exclusively on what he is saying and defer his own meditations. But he finds that quite impossible. He is getting more bored by the day, finds the play drearier; he's never had such a boring part. It is of no help to him whatsoever that the play has been so successful. He knows the play is a con. Initially, he'd not thought that, had believed passionately in the work. He was thrilled with the role! He remembers the day they called him, the evening he read the play, from beginning to end in one sitting, his return call to the director that same night, enthusiastically accepting the role. But now with each performance he realizes there is nothing behind the glitter of the words. However much the critics analyzed the play, and (in a rare show of unanimity) all had praised it, however much the audiences packed the theatre every day, and there'd been a flood of invitations to tour the play abroad, it had gone flat as far as he was concerned. No one knew it as well as he did. Not counting the rehearsals (that lasted months), he had performed it nine-hundred-and-twenty-three times. Today was number nine-hundred-and-twenty-four. And after nine-hundred-and-twenty-four performances one knows a work back to front. One knows that, if it were any good, one would have reached that number without any problems: after the nine-hundred-and-twen-ty-fourth or fifteen-thousand-and-thirteenth, he would have contin-ued to find new insights. When it comes to bad plays, on the other hand, each performance reveals a new crack. After nine hundred and twenty-four performances, the cracks win out and the play falls flat. No matter that nobody, except him, notices. Like this obediently laughing audience, laughing precisely in the silence marked out for laughter. As soon as the laughs end, he resumes the monologue and, speaking all the time, sits on a chair, puts his elbows on the table, and places his head in his hands. He has repeated this action so often . . . Instead of sitting down and placing his head in his hands, why doesn't he, one night, go to the curtain and smell it, or lift his foot up and examine the sole of his shoe? He has repeated it all so often he could perform the play (from the first to the last scene) in total darkness, on a stage that had been turned into a minefield. A suitably mined stage would be no problem for a methodical actor—he could tread fearlessly there, confident he'd never step on a mine, every movement would be etched on his brain, to the last millimeter. Today's actors are undisciplined; they modify their movements from one performance to the next, not to improve them (no problem, if improvement were the aim) but because of their lack of discipline—they'd be blown up after taking a few steps. Hah! He simulates a coughing attack, spits out the last sentences of his monologue, hits his fist against the blue and green flowery wallpaper (gently, even though the sound echoes round the auditorium), and sits down again. When he finishes the monologue, with the words "If it weren't for that, all would have been in vain!", the actress will makes her entrance (she is thrilled by the work and will never, however many years pass, realize that it is completely devoid of substance), will simulate surprise and say: "Hi, Lluc. I didn't expect to find you here." The actor hears footsteps, feigns surprise, stands up, and concludes: "If it weren't for that, all would have been in vain!" The actress immediately makes her entrance and says: "Hi, Lluc. I didn't expect to find you here." The actor walks over to her, not exactly gracefully, embraces her, she rejects him histrionically, he retreats to the sideboard and decides to abandon ship: to make an announcement that very day, as soon as this performance is over, to the effect that he no longer finds the play fulfilling, that he needs fresh, intelligent challenges. But what excuse can he give? He can't say, just like that, without further explanation, that he's abandoning a work he has performed, without interruption, for years, the work which has finally, after decades of struggle, brought him fame and recognition. He can't confess that he's gradually discovered that the work he was so proud of performing, nine-hundred-and-twenty-four times, is complete garbage. If he pretends to be sick (actor and actress now kiss passionately), the performances would be suspended. But how long could he pretend to be sick before the impresario started to suspect something? A fortnight? A month? If his fake illness lasted any longer, the impresario (despite himself, even though he doesn't suspect foul play) would look for a replacement. The play has reached its climax. It can't be suspended just like that. After the kiss, the actress ostentatiously cleans her lips on the back of her hand and rebukes him; he insults her, imagines his substitute playing the role he has made famous (not for a moment does he consider the possibility *he* might do it better); the very thought makes him shudder. He also shudders when he thinks that's the only reason he doesn't leave and continues performing the role day after day, and when the curtain falls and he hears the audience applaud, he gives a routine wave, full of pride.

The Lives
of the
Prophets

The man gets up, eyes sparkling, breathing feverishly, with one aim in mind: to reveal to the world what has just been revealed to him. He rubs his eyes; the revelation is still crystal clear. Until this moment, he would have found it difficult to accept that he could suddenly become a prophet. Now, on the contrary, he discovers he can assume the role with the requisite faith and *sang-froid*. As he hurries downstairs in his pajamas (his mission is too momentous to worry about trivial details like finding his pants, shirt, and jacket), the trumpet blasts still echoing round his head, he sees his wife in the kitchen getting breakfast ready and their child bawling in his cot. His wife is surprised to see him up so early. She tells him so, but he doesn't hear her because he's already opening their front door and stepping out into the street, determined to divulge his revelation. He reaches the square, sees a green Volkswagen Passat parked next to the bakery, and climbs on top. It is the perfect pulpit. The four individuals who have come out to buy bread, savory pastries, or milk for breakfast (wrapped up tight, wearing scarves and hats pulled down over their ears) look at him bleary-eyed. He is sporting sky-blue, gray-striped pajamas; the wind sears his skin and freezes his bones. Wasting no time, he takes a deep breath, stares at the glazed faces of the four individuals staring up at him (one man's nibbling the crust of a baguette he's carrying under his arm), and goes blank. What was he supposed to be prophesying? He can't remember.

The more stressed he gets, because he can't remember, the blanker his brain becomes. Time rushes by. People look at him, rooted to the spot, and he finds that even more stressful. Was what he had to prophesy good or evil? It was mind blowing, for sure: he *can* remember how he reacted. But was it a mind-blowing reaction to good or to evil? And hadn't he felt quite shocked? Had it perhaps fallen to him to prophesy the horrific end of the world? No, it wasn't anything like that. Was it the opposite, a new dawn of hope? Too grandiose. It was no earth-shaking prophecy. Perhaps it was more modest. But what was it? He can hear the sound of a TV from a nearby window. A dance orchestra is playing a musical interlude on the morning program. He tries to concentrate and remember at last what it was. But it's not coming. Seconds pass as if they were minutes, the four people who were looking at him drift away (one by one), and he's left standing there with his finger sticking up and his mouth open, speechless. Until the owner of the Volkswagen appears, surprised to see a man on top of his car, and angrily bawls him off the hood; then he grabs the prophet by the lapels and slams him up against the wall, while the prophet tries (in vain) to remember whether that was what he had to prophesy, being knocked against the wall, being in a state of uncertainty, being unable to remember.

He ruminated for days. He was absolutely clear on one front: he had *not* deceived himself into thinking he had something to prophesy when, in fact, there was nothing. His gut feeling was right. He had been summoned to prophesy an extraordinary occurrence. But was it extraordinary for the world? Or simply for him? That was why he had run downstairs and into the street, so he could bring it into the open. But could he still remember what it was when he was on his way downstairs, or did he come down awestruck, remembering nothing, yet obsessed by the need to tell everyone?

How can one forget a revelation? One can forget something normal that any mortal might know, a simple piece of information or an item one has discovered or got by paying cash: a name, the plot of a film, or an umbrella. But not a prophecy. This makes him realize how deceptive one's memory can be and forces him to contemplate the possibility that it was not so much a prophecy as a dream. A dream that had seemed so real he had *mistaken* it for a prophecy. But he knows it wasn't a dream. And also knows that if he doesn't manage to remember, he will feel eternally mortified. His wife taunts him at every opportunity: "What kind of prophet are you? If you can't remember the prophecy, there was no such thing. Ezekiel and Isaiah would never have been prophets if they'd forgotten what they were supposed to be prophesying. That would have been hilarious, for sure. Can you imagine them saying they'd forgotten?"

"What if a prophet suffered from memory loss? That's hardly his fault. I can even agree that I am a bad prophet, a clueless or mediocre prophet. But in either case I am a prophet. A truth *was* revealed to me. I know that is the case and I'm not deceiving myself. That fact isn't belied by my lapses of memory. I will remember some day. But even if I can't, it's nothing unusual. Nobody can deprive me of my role simply because there's never been an absent-minded prophet before. There'd never been a prophet who flew off in a chariot of fire until one did just that."

The prophetic state can be a spontaneous happening or be prompted by a variety of techniques: meditation, magical or mystical formulas, movements or punishment of the body. Also by music, particularly drums. Or by dancing or ingesting narcotics. Maybe, thinks the prophet, he should stimulate himself, take recourse to one of these methods. He is increasingly clear that what's really serious is not that he has forgotten what he should be prophesying, but his inability to put it all behind him. This makes him feel even more exasperated, sinks him into a mood of deep despondency, and makes him finally suspect that the revelation that caused him to get up, eyes sparkling, breathing feverishly, was exactly that, after the initial epiphany, he wouldn't remember anything at all when he was out in the street.

A few years later, out of the blue, the prophet feels another revelation coming on. The trumpet blasts, the dazzling flashes of light, the words intoned clearly and slowly by a solemn voice. He had read that prophecies *can* be repeated, particularly in the case of prophets who feel reluctant to assume their role. To ensure this prophecy doesn't elude him, he switches on his bedside lamp and looks for paper and pencil in his drawer. He can't find either. He jumps out of bed. He can't find either in his whole bedroom. He rushes into the kitchen; there's a notepad hanging on the wall, in the shape of a chef wearing his hat: the pad is his apron. But when he gets there he sees that the pad is used up and the chef is displaying an obscene hole rather than an apron of sheets of paper. He'd forgotten. The pad had run out days ago and he hadn't remembered to buy a new one, precisely because there hadn't been any paper left to jot down a reminder to buy a new pad. This lack of coherence really winds the prophet up. Shouldn't notepads have an end paper, where one can jot down a reminder to buy a new notepad? Sure enough the pad's last page should, to a certain extent, fulfill this function. But how can we know that we're writing on the last sheet if nothing identifies it as such? There could very well be one underneath. To ensure users know it's the last one, at a glance, the solution would be to make it a different color: yellow, pale green, bluish, light enough to write on with the usual pens or pencils but distinct from the last white page, so one realizes it is the end sheet and jots down: "Buy another notepad." They could even carry a message, like those calendars that tell you in mid-December: "Buy this or that new calendar," understanding by "this or that" the brand of the calendar in question. Evidently this last sheet would increase the item's price (because of the different color or extra printing), but this increase would be easily offset by the advantages of having the sheet. This final sheet would be similar to the sheet one finds in a checkbook, the one that indicates the checkbook is almost used up and that one should ask one's bank for a new one.

The prophet is thinking all this while searching anxiously for a scrap of paper to jot down his revelation. But even before finding one (he finds a notebook in his son's briefcase and tears a sheet out), he knows that when he finally has that sheet in front of him, and his pen (he takes one from the pencil case in the same briefcase), so much time will have passed and he will be so stressed out that he'll forget what it was yet again. In effect, when he has the sheet in front of him and a pen at the ready, he can't remember the revelation. Only shards, fragments, and vague ideas remain. But he finds it impossible to reconstruct. Besides, he's wracked by doubt. Was this revelation the same as the last one or were they two distinct revelations? Has God repeated the message he'd not been able to remember, or did He decide it was a lost cause and send him a new one?

The day after he decides to put a notebook and pen on his bedside table, just in case, the revelation is repeated. Obviously he regrets forgetting it again, but he finds the fact he has had another revelation hugely encouraging; we can assert that he's never been as optimistic as he is today. Because this second revelation confirms he is a genuine prophet. His only idiosyncrasy is that he has a bad memory. Another source of hope: if the revelation has been repeated once, it can be repeated again.

He buys a small cassette-recorder in an electronics shop; he always carries it with him and puts it on his bedside table at night, ready to switch it on as soon as he has another revelation: if he sees it's going to elude him yet again, he'll record it rather than write it down. Even so, he keeps the notebook and pencil nearby, in case the cassette recorder doesn't work or the batteries run out, even though he checks them every week, and he throws them away and inserts new ones long before they run out.

The years go by, but all his precautions are in vain. He has no more revelations. That son who was in his cot when he had his first one is now twenty-eight years old. His father has alerted him: You could get a surprise at any time, and you must always be prepared. When he was seven, his mother died; father and son wondered for several days whether that could have possibly been the prophecy, that his mother would die and he'd be half-orphaned. But it didn't strike any bells with his father. Even so, they kept wondering. Whenever a war broke out or there was a disaster somewhere in the world, father and son wondered whether that might not be what had been revealed.

The father is now on his deathbed and calls for his son. His son is sitting outside on a chair, head bowed. The doctor leaves the bedroom, tells him to go in and to be sure, above all, not to tire him. The son enters the bedroom in a highly emotional state. The prophet's eyes sparkle; he tries to talk, but is exhausted. He tries to say something, is breathless, takes a deep breath, closes his eyes for a moment, as if keeping them open was a struggle, but then re-opens them immediately. He says: "Son . . ."; his son leans over, clasps his father's right hand in both of his. "Before I die . . ." the prophet whispers. But he immediately goes silent again. He looks away and stares at the opposite wall. His son looks where his father is looking, in case there is some special sign, some thing to indicate what he is trying to say with those quavering words, evidently the last words he will ever say, his final farewell. The son squeezes his father's hand even harder. "Rest. Don't try to say anything." The prophet suddenly feels a breath of energy. "I mean that . . ." The door opens, and the nurse clatters in on her heels. The voice of the dying man is lost in the racket. The son puts his ear to his father's mouth, hopes he will repeat himself. The nurse changes the bottle on the drip that enters one of the dying man's veins through a tube. The son is literally lying on top of his father. Once she has changed the bottle, the nurse leaves, trying to ensure that her heels don't clatter as much as they did when she came in. The prophet opens his eyes again. When he yawns, there are grayish folds at the corners of his mouth. "That's why . . ." "Don't force yourself . . ." ". . . I didn't know how to . . ."

The old man closes his eyes and breathes with difficulty. What *is* he trying to tell him? Could he have remembered the prophecy on his deathbed? "Now I want to tell you . . ." The dying man opens his eyes wide, opens his mouth wide, and stiffens. His son sobs. He leaves the bedroom and looks for the doctor. The doctor certifies that he is dead. He lowers the eyelids with tweezers. The son leaves the bedroom. Other relatives in the dining room stop him and embrace him. One scene of grief follows another. He receives condolences, hugs shoulders, shakes hands, and wipes away his and other people's tears. Throughout his life, the family had rarely talked about his father's status as a prophet, and at that moment the son intuits a vague glint of curiosity in the occasional look, an interest in whether his father had remembered any of his revelations in the last seconds of his life.

Someone had made coffee in the kitchen. The son pours himself a cup. He takes small sips because it's burning hot. His relatives keep hugging him. He looks for a place where he can be alone. He decides to hide in the lobby. Nobody will see him in the darkness there, and he can be by himself for a few moments. As he heads that way, a cousin sees him from afar, walks over, gives him a hug, and inquires after his mental state. When the cousin goes back inside, the son opens the door on to the landing, walks out, and shuts it behind him, trying not to make any noise that might alert the others. He walks down the stairs and out into the street.

- 2 -

He finds work in another city. It's a good idea to move and live in another city. They sell his father's house, and he leaves. He establishes his own business a few months later with two work colleagues. He has a reasonable standard of living, is relatively happy, and plays cards with friends on Friday nights.

He wakes up one cold winter's morning with a vision of a city in flames, its buildings in ruins, its roads full of deep fissures and people fleeing, panic-stricken. The images speed by at an unlikely rate and are accompanied by trumpet blasts. It is a very short, intense vision, and he strives to remember what's written in white on a green and blue sign: PLACE LACHAMBAUDIE. The sign is the size and color of a Parisian street-sign. If he had a guide, he would check whether a square called Lachambaudie existed in Paris.

The next day he goes to a bookshop and buys a street guide to Paris: *Guide general de Paris. Répertoire des rues. Éditions L'Indispensable.* As he's taking the guide out of the bag in the shop doorway and looking for Lachambaudie on the alphabetical list of squares, he hears the word "earthquake" on the lips of one of the girls walking into the shop at that moment. He turns around, goes over to them, apologizes for intruding, and asks which earthquake they are talking about. One of them says the earthquake that hit Paris two hours ago. The prophet's son breaks into a run. He stops in front of an electronics shop and sees a Paris that has fallen victim to an earthquake, that not even the detectors had foreseen, on a dozen televisions.

He feels guilty that he said nothing. He watches them pulling corpses out of the rubble a thousand kilometers away and thinks he made a big mistake not telling any of the powers-that-be and wasting a regrettable amount of time looking for a street guide to check whether a square by the name of Lachambaudie existed in Paris. He only calms down when he realizes that if he had, nobody would have believed him and all those people would have died anyway.

A year and a half later, also in the early morning, he sees (for tenths of a second, also with trumpets blasting) a terrible epidemic that in a matter of weeks ravages a country he can't identify (he thinks it's in Asia). He immediately speaks to the health authorities, so as not to repeat his negligence over his vision of the Paris earthquake. He tells them about the precedent of his father, how he foresaw the Paris earthquake, and how that tragedy took place because he'd said nothing. They say thank you very much and take notes, but he knows they're only humoring him; basically they don't believe a word.

A week later, the newspapers are filled with nothing else but reports of mortality rates in Laos and Cambodia. Ninety-eight percent of the population of Laos and twenty per cent of Cambodia's have already died. Months later, by the time the epidemic is under control, Laos, Cambodia, and half of Thailand have been devastated.

A year after, he wakes up one morning and (the same few tenths of a second and usual trumpet blasts) sees a school bus tumbling off of a cliff. He knows which school it is because the name's written in large spindly letters across the top of the windshield. He rushes off to talk to the school's headmaster. He describes his vision: the bus, the road, and the bend with the ravine. The headmaster is impressed; the bus always drives along the road he saw in his dream, and around the bend with the drop into a ravine. He calls the driver in and tells him. When the prophet's son sees him (a prophet now, indeed, on his own merits), he whistles. It's the man who is driving the bus when it tumbles into the ravine. The headmaster is really impressed yet again, and very grateful. But on which day did it happen? The prophet can't say for sure. The headmaster takes a decision: the bus will follow an alternative route for a time, and a new driver will replace the usual one.

Two months later, as the predicted calamity hasn't happened, the usual driver returns, but as a precaution, he will follow the alternative route. After six months, given it is impossible to continue taking the much longer, costlier route, he returns to the traditional one. When he is close to the bend by the ravine, the driver takes even more care than usual. Weeks and months pass without any problems. At the very beginning of June, the bus hurtles into the ravine.

People look at him maliciously, as if he were in some way guilty. One evening, the police had to stop the relatives of the dead children from lynching him. The prophet tells them time and again that they are confusing prophesying an event with causing it. The headmaster agrees. And he too feels vaguely, unjustifiably guilty. What should he have done? Change the route for all time? Fire the driver without good reason? Nothing tangible indicated that the accident was inevitable.

The prophet reproaches himself. Months later, one morning when the trumpets and dazzling lights reveal to him that the British Airways flight 5397 from Barcelona to Birmingham will crash, he decides to say nothing. However much they try to stop it, the accident is bound to take place. If he predicts it, people will think he is in good measure responsible. But he finds it difficult to have that knowledge and keep it to himself. Besides, in this case, the solution seems simple enough. If the Barcelona-Birmingham flight that is going to crash is the 5397, all they have to do is change the number 5397 and give the flight a number than nobody uses (for example, 7612): numbers can't be in short supply. However, is it possible to short-circuit a prediction? He can't sleep knowing deaths could be avoided by taking such a simple step as changing the flight number. If the company would listen to him, the problem would be solved. He informs the company, tells them his record of prophecies and the vision he has had about flight 5397. The directors of the company give him a pleasant welcome and tell him that if they paid attention to everyone who claimed they had a presentiment that such and such a flight will be involved in an accident, they wouldn't be able to fly anywhere. Years ago they took the decision to ignore them systematically.

Now that the situation is out in the open, the prophet tells a newspaper (the only daily, a sensationalist rag, that will listen) what has happened, his record of prophecies and the precedent of his father, and warns that, if the company persists in ignoring him, the 5397 flight from Barcelona to Birmingham is going to have an accident. The daily, it's short on space, publishes the news (bottom half of the left-hand page) and calls the prophet a half-mad lunatic. When the plane crashes three days later, the disaster brings him public recognition. Opinion champions him and turns against the air company. How could they have scorned a prediction that was so clear, that would have made the accident so easy to avoid? The newspapers that hadn't showed the slightest interest in his story before the crash now want to interview him. In every single interview, the final question is about whether he has new predictions to make. A journalist on the country's second most important daily makes fun of the fact that people keep talking about prophecies when it is obvious they are simply visions. A prophecy is much more elevated and transcendent. The prophet emphasizes that the importance of what is being revealed to him doesn't warrant any divisive pigeonholing. It is no less crucial if it is of worldwide or simply individual interest: it is a revelation of a future event, and this is all that matters. Indeed, perhaps his father never remembered his revelations because he persisted in trying to discern something that was universally valuable, an element of redemption.

The prophet is now so famous that when he has his next revelation (that a particular cruiser on a Christmas cruise around the islands of the Aegean is going to sink), the authorities decide to believe him. They don't cancel the cruise, but they don't allow any passengers on board. And when the vessel shipwrecks, it does so in the glare of television cameras that are broadcasting every moment of the ship sinking and the rescue of the crew by helicopters that were accompanying the ship expressly for that purpose. Immediately afterwards, he prophesies a new war between two countries in South America, but not even the big powers can do anything to prevent that, and war breaks out. He predicts a *tsunami* that will bring destruction to Chile, Hawaii, and Japan. He predicts trains will collide near Bologna and the imminent death of the king of Norway. When he foresees the eruption of a volcano near the island of Mexcala, in Lake Chapala, the authorities quickly evacuate the area and the loss of human life is nil, although nearby villages are devastated by the lava. He's now being asked to predict everything: if such a day would be good for elections, if such a place is ideal for building a new airport, what the future holds for such and such a prime minister. He feels he is being treated like an oracle. People stop him in the street and ask him what the weather's going to be like on the weekend or the number that's going to win the next lottery. Time and again he has to make it clear that he knows nothing about most things, that he can only prophesy what has been revealed to him. The journalists who imagine him making predictions à la carte find this most disappointing.

When a bomb explodes in the train station for the Berlin zoo (seventy-nine fatalities), the news is on every front page and all eyes are turned on him. Why didn't he foresee it? Once again, he has to remind people that he has no power over which events will be revealed to him and which won't, and no way of intuiting beyond what he is shown in the revelation. Nevertheless, however often he tells people, from then on, some individuals (including the journalist who believes he is more a visionary than a prophet) reproach him for every event he doesn't predict, particularly if it's a catastrophe. "Perhaps we shall never know what his hidden reasons for not predicting this event were," one article on the bombing of the Berlin station concluded, almost accusing him of conniving with the terrorists. The headline was: "A prophet when it suits."

The prophet goes on predicting: peace between the two countries warring in South America, the murder of the Dutch prime minister, the fall of such and such an African dictatorship, the imminent creation of a definitive vaccination against the new lethal strain of hepatitis that appeared three years ago. The same trumpets are blasting, but the revelations are completely random. One day in September it's even revealed to him which team will win La Liga. Criticisms rain down on him for being trivial and frivolous and "abusing his prestige as a prophet." The frequency of his revelations increases. Until he can't avoid predicting almost everything and knowing what will happen at any moment. He meets a girl, and before he's spoken to her, he knows it is going to end badly for one reason or another. With one it's because he can't stand being jealous (it's especially gruesome, because the girl's repeated infidelities are revealed to him in all their gory detail). With another, it's because she's soon sick to death of so many visions. The gift of prophecy prevents him from leading a normal life. When he meets Marta he knows (the next Saturday, in an early morning revelation, with Marta by his side) that he'll marry her, that they will have son and will separate a few months after he is born. He also knows that, before that, time will move on, they will buy a green Rover, license plate 4436 BKR, six months later their neighbor will have an accident at home, three years later they will eat Christmas dinner in Can Nofre, his sister-in-law will unexpectedly drop by the day after, and he will be bored to tears for the rest of his life.

His son is a month old. He gives him his bottle, puts him in his cot, gets into bed, and, before falling asleep, suddenly hears, like almost every morning, the sound of trumpets. They have become so routine they no longer excite him. He opens his left eye. He is so sleepy; the last thing he feels like right now is another revelation—he'd give anything to be able to ignore it and get some shut-eye. Nobody gets a decent night's sleep when it's bottle-time every three hours. But he can't do anything: the bright lights are flashing before his eyes, and slowly and solemnly, a totally unexpected revelation appears: he will *never* have another revelation.

It leaves him cold. Better that way, he thinks. At last he will be able to relax, at last he will be the same as other people, at last he is going lead a normal life, like the rest of humanity. He falls asleep hugging his pillow but wakes up before dawn, panic-stricken. What will he do with his life from now on? Not having any more revelations is all well and good, sleeping in the early morning, or relaxing in a bar, without having a visitation from trumpet blasts or dazzling lights. He now has to face the fact that, without noticing, he has been constructing his life around this special talent of his. Without the gift of prophecy, how will he confront a world that expects him to make new prophecies every day? What will he do, if he ceases to be a prophet?

He decides to pretend. For a time, he says nothing to anyone. He predicts nothing. He forecasts nothing. Months fly by and people begin to complain that he is no longer making prophecies. He first uses his child as the excuse: young kids are lots of work and you can't do anything else. Then he tries to pass off obviously inevitable events as prophecies events. On such a day in such a place the sun is going to vanish. But the ruse doesn't work: because everyone knows that on such a day in such a place there will be an eclipse.

One morning he opens the picture windows of his house (there's always a group of journalists below, armed with cameras and cassette recorders, ready to record his every word), and in a grandiloquent tone he says he has just had a revelation: the world will come to an end—he has seen a vision of a barren, lifeless, devastated planet. The revelation doesn't stir even the most ardent believers in the apocalypse. "We know the world will end one day or another. Pompous assertions like this are no use to us," writes a journalist, who had previously reproached him for his simplicity and the downbeat nature of his revelations. People gradually start to make fun of him and come out with pithy put-downs. "He's lost it." This happens at a time when Marta tells him he's never been a good husband and has always been obsessed by his visions, by his petty, egocentric world as a prophet, a world that's now evidently coming to an end. She tells him she's reached a decision: she's leaving him and taking their son with her. This is the last prophecy to be fulfilled. The prophet had foreseen it, but regrettably never said anything to anyone, not even Marta. If he did so now, he would still retain a minimal, threadbare credibility.

After seeing how soon people forget, oblivion takes him by surprise. He'd never have imagined, when the moment came, that he would miss people's (should he say the public's) warmth so much. He opens his window, and there aren't any journalists waiting, cameras and cassette-recorders at the ready. He had wanted to lead a normal, anonymous life, but now he misses the limelight and wants to defer the dreadful moment, in whatever way possible. If only he could tell them the truth . . . That he's had a revelation: he will *never* again have another revelation. It's not a bad idea. But it's too late now. If he'd told people when it came to him, it would have made the front pages, and he could have beat a dignified retreat. Just imagine the headlines: "His last prophecy before bidding a definitive farewell is that he will *never* have another revelation." But it's too late. To reveal that now would be an admission of failure. And to avoid admitting that he is a complete failure, to deny that he'd been one for years, he takes the plane to Berlin one day, checks in at a hotel (the Berlin Steigenberger, near the zoo), and immediately goes out for a stroll. The next day he will let it be known he has another prediction to reveal. He's greeted with skepticism. "Wonder whether it's going to be 'in two years time June 23rd will fall on a Wednesday' kind."

Like in the old days, the prophet is back in a press conference. He says hello to a journalist who interviewed him years ago, when there were seventy-nine fatalities. He declares he's had a revelation. The train station for the Berlin zoo is going to be blown up. Some people protest: That's no prophecy; it happened years ago when, in fact, he didn't foresee it. The prophet says this is a completely new revelation. They ask him when it's going to happen and how. He replies it will happen that afternoon. The authorities react immediately. Like in the old days, they don't doubt the veracity of what he's said for a second and take the necessary security measures. Shortly before two o'clock, at the head of a crowd of police and journalists, the prophet enters the train station to show them where the most frightening devastation and flames occurred in his revelation. That very instant the bombs explode, one after another.

During
the War

War broke out mid-morning. At half past eleven the situation was confused, and by midday the sense of uncertainty was (depending where and how one was situated) absolute; the lack of clear demarcations between the factions (and the various, often ideologically opposed groups that were behind each of these factions that were sometimes at loggerheads, thus creating new splinter groups) contributed to the confusion, as did the fact that a certain percentage of the population that had cottoned on (the war, so often anticipated *sotto voce*, was now a reality) didn't know exactly what attitude to adopt. There was another percentage (overwhelmingly the majority) that acted as if nothing had happened and everything was completely normal, though their motives weren't entirely clear; the nature of the conflict encouraged their stance: equivocal and oracular poses that meant they didn't express themselves as exuberantly as usual. There were no troops on the streets or barricades in the avenues. No parades or harangues. Military garrisons maintained a (ostensibly ostensible) calm, concealing, it wasn't difficult to intuit, a state of high agitation. The nervousness of military command was clear in their hastily given orders, which were imbued with an excessively heightened sense of conviction, and the wave of orders and counter-orders that was so complex it revealed their underlying insecurity. All that calm (if one could use that word), all that suspicious normality simply indicated the hostility in the air.

At midday, though summoned by nobody, simply moved by their civic instincts and anxiety, those citizens who were conscious of the situation started to head towards the square, wanting to find out what was really going on. According to some, the trigger had been a revolt (it was unclear whether it was military or civilian) in a distant province (it was unspecified and varied from mouth to mouth: it was this or that depending on the speaker), a revolt that had been seething for months. Its distance from the centers of power was one of the reasons why no untoward developments were in evidence in the capital (said those returning from there). According to others, in principle it involved a confrontation between two factions (that weren't openly antagonistic) within the army, an army that in the past had won victories and accomplished feats that had become legendary and that, until very recently, had enjoyed a generous budget, though a degree of unease had been generated in the higher ranks that resulted from the economic restrictions they now faced, inactivity, and restrictions encouraged by the absence of bellicose conflicts of any significance, whether inside or outside the country. However, according to others, there had been a coup d'état in the capital (led by whom?), kept under wraps as much by its instigators (convinced that the most effective coup d'état was the least noticed) as by its victims, who considered that their best option, given that the coup leaders weren't intending to glory in it, was to maintain a prudent silence, thus sparing themselves from having to admit defeat. So they acted as if nothing had happened, which meant they ensured that most of the population and diplomatic missions continued to be in the dark (or at least acted as if they were), to such an extent that if anyone decided to publicly insinuate that something was wrong, they would point to the calm on the streets to support their case. The coup's leaders and the deposed leaders were then theoretically, and paradoxically, in accord. The fact that the pact of silence was supported equally on both sides meant that other people, who were even more devious, imagined that the coup's leaders and the deposed leaders had planned everything down to the smallest detail, so the coup would go completely unnoticed. Given the silence, that seemed to have no apparent fissures, how could the engaged citizens properly evaluate the facts? The radio wasn't broadcasting only classical music, as was usual in such circumstances, and the television continued with its planned schedule. At that very moment a film was coming to an end—part of the Elvis Presley cycle that had begun three weeks ago: Elvis Presley dives into the water, people applaud, Elvis swims to the cliff, climbs up, dries himself on a towel, and gets dressed. A crowd of men carries him on their shoulders back to the hotel. Everybody congratulates him; Ursula Andress says: "Bravo," they kiss, are surrounded by a mariachi band, and Elvis breaks into song. Following the Elvis film, the program schedule continued as planned (this was particularly significant) and no reference was made to any conflict. Consequently, the engaged citizens found themselves deprived of the data that was necessary to evaluate the real situation; a lack of orientation that only increased their doubts and caused misgivings and rumors to spread like wildfire. Such a tenuous basis in fact precipitated a moment when people quickly flitted from one supposition to another, leading to a third that opened the way to a fourth, each as impossible to prove as any of the preceding ones yet accepted as readily as any accomplished fact. And had there been lots of casualties, as someone claimed? Was the situation changing drastically, as another reported? And, besides, was changing drastically in relation to *which* previous situation? The tensions between the engaged citizens heightened, fanned by their different perspectives and inability to prove a thing, which prevented them from reaching any decision, specific or not. In demonstrations in front of the military government building, the tension caused by this dearth of data would often seethe to a metaphorical boiling point, and the most incensed citizens had to be pulled apart from the most phlegmatic of the citizenry. There were those who even questioned whether it was necessary to take a decision. Why should they? Wasn't it better to carry on as they were? (Obviously, with their ears to the ground. They could all agree on that.) The arguments became so acrimonious that at 2:00 P.M. it was finally decided to defer any decision till after lunch, so they could debate more calmly. Everyone went home, except for three citizens who always went out for lunch; they headed to a nearby restaurant. The situation was no less tense inside: whispering around every table, averted gazes, and dissimulation.

In mid-afternoon, troop movements were detected in front of the military government building. However, right away, those who question everything made their voices heard: Was there any indication, any particular sign of aggression in those movements? Could one deduce that something really serious was afoot, or were they simply routine drills? Barely accustomed to army maneuvers, the engaged citizens (who'd now lunched, met in the café, and made their leisurely way to the military government building) hadn't a clue how to interpret them; they could all agree on that. A black car, with a black pennant, drove up at 4:32. An officer got out. From that distance, most of the engaged citizens, who'd been conscientious objectors, were unable to define his exact rank. Was he a general? A captain-general? A lieutenant-general? Or a mere lieutenant? Would it have given them a clue, had they known? It obviously wouldn't have, and this made them even more irate—anger they directed at themselves on this occasion. They thought that the two sentries (doing their duty on either side of the main entrance, in concrete boxes with green-tiled domes) saluted him particularly respectfully, but people weren't unanimous about that. Once the officer had entered the building, the car drove off. Did its immediate departure denote anything serious, or on the contrary, was it a positive sign? At 6:32, a demonstration of engineering workers in overalls walked up High Street and into the square. The demonstration had been called the previous week, complied with all the legal requirements, and was, thus, totally authorized. Once again, the rumor mill found fresh proof in the fact that none of the powers-that-be (whether civilian or military) had banned it: if it had been banned, it would have been a sign, an acknowledgement of the anomalous situation. They could agree on that. Consequently, they let the demonstration go ahead, and some 150 individuals (a hundred, according to the report filed by the municipal police) marched to the West Bridge, without hindrance: there they dispersed peacefully, heading home or to the nearest watering-holes. Suddenly, at 7:13, the same officer who had alighted from the car a few hours earlier came out of the military government building. However, he was now in the company of another officer of a different rank, but again those present couldn't determine what his rank was due to the aforementioned gap in their knowledge. The car (the same one from earlier in the afternoon; a citizen with a fine memory had memorized the license plate number) was waiting for them.

It would be a tense night. The hours passed slowly. The engaged citizens twisted and turned sleeplessly in their beds. How could they sleep when they felt so anxious? Radio stations still weren't broadcasting classical music and the television kept to its scheduled programs: a competition with couples who'd broken up and the next chapter in a television drama, which that night revealed that one of the characters was a homosexual.

Calm in the night. Carousing in bars, the early morning din of the trash collectors. At half past six the shutters at the kiosks started going up. At 10:00 A.M. (barely twenty-four hours after this had all begun!), the first cannonades were heard. Twenty-one, to be precise. There we go. The engaged citizens immediately went out into the street; some sought shelter in the nearest subway stations, mingling with less conscious citizens who were apparently continuing their normal daily lives. After the twenty-one cannonades, silence. The midday television news reported that the prime minister of an economic, political, and military power of the highest level had arrived in the city that morning. This visit provoked contrary opinions among the aware citizenry. Some believed the visit was an excuse to cover up the cannonades they had heard that morning (on the pretext that they were in his honor). Others reckoned the visit wasn't gratuitous or innocent (nothing is, never ever) and that the great power was attempting either to mediate in the conflict (sheer effrontery) or help one side (absolutely intolerable interference, whichever side they were trying to help). In the afternoon, the first casualties were announced: a five-a-side rugby game in the Olympic Stadium ended with seven injured when supporters of both sides fought a pitched battle on the terraces. Shortly afterwards, it was evening, anguish, and nighttime. The pattern was repeated, day after day, for weeks, with small variations that introduced fresh doubts, fresh evidence, and fresh uncertainties. The drama didn't lie in the number of deaths (so well concealed as to seem non-existent), the distraught families (these were few in number, prompted by motives unrelated to the conflict), the homes abandoned, or hunger (these had been a factor for years) as much as in the withholding of breath, the wild hypothesizing, and the futile attempts to find out what was really happening. They spent months weighing up new hypotheses and finally found themselves back where they had started: awash in what they themselves ironically dubbed a sea of disinformation. And not the slightest expression of solidarity from any other country, far or near. They found this cold-shouldering by the outside world even more depressing.

Would that war last forever? There'd been one that had even lasted a hundred years that the history books still debated with a sickening indifference. They needed another ninety-eight to equal that war. Humanity's ability to adapt is admirable. Faced by these rather bleak prospects, parents opted to enlighten their offspring and prepare them for life in such conditions. Generation followed generation, and the parents of the engaged citizenry passed the arguments that were necessary for survival in that unending war on to their children, the first being to keep quiet and adopt an outlook of complete indifference, like every other citizen.

Until, one day when the younger element among the aware citizenry couldn't agree which year everything had begun (obviously encyclopedias and history books were silent on the matter and portrayed those years as a period of peace and splendor). There was one particularly independent, iconoclastic youth who kicked open the door of the cafeteria, where they met each Tuesday and Thursday to find out about the latest state of play, walked to the table where they were all prevaricating, and told them the news: the war had finished as unexpectedly as it had begun—that afternoon at 5:34. The most cheerful, ingenuous citizens gave a sigh of relief, but the most aware of the aware lowered their heads in sorrow. Because, if a war is hard enough, the post-war period that inevitably follows is even harder and that peace (signed in unimaginable conditions with unimaginable burdens for the citizenry that the media obsessively concealed) was an ineluctable indicator that the post-war period had started.

Books

There are four books on the passionate reader's table. All waiting to be read. He went to the bookshop this afternoon, and after spending an hour around the new releases tables and reviewing the covers of his favorite authors on the shelves, he chose four. One is a book of short stories by a French writer; he really enjoyed a novel of his years ago. He didn't like the second novel he published that much (in fact, didn't like it all) and has now bought this book of stories in the hope of re-discovering what had fired his imagination so many years ago. The second book is a novel by a Dutch writer whose two preceding novels he had tried to read, but with little success, because he'd had to put both of them down after a few lines. Strangely, this didn't lead him to abandon the idea of a fresh attempt. Strangely, because usually, when he can't stand twenty lines of the first book by a particular writer, he might try the second but never the third, unless the critics he trusts have singled it out for special praise, or a friend has recommended it particularly enthusiastically. But this wasn't the case now. Why did he decide to give him another try? Perhaps it's the beginning. The beginning that goes: "The bellhop rushed in shouting: "Mr. Kington! Mr. Kington, please!" Mr.

Kington was reading the newspaper in the lobby of the Ambassade Hotel and was about to raise his hand when he realized that nobody, but nobody, knew he was there. He didn't even look up when the bellhop walked by. It would be the most intelligent decision he had ever taken."

The third book is also a novel, the first novel by an American author he has never heard of. He bought it because in spite of the initial quotation ("Oh, how the tiles glinted in the blossoming dawn, when the roosters' cry broke the silence with the sound . . .") he had leafed through it and felt drawn in. The fourth book is a book of short stories, also by a Dutch writer, one who had been unpublished to that point. What attracted him to that book? If he were to be sincere, it was the rich abundance of initials: there are three (A., F., Th.) before the three words that make up the surname. A total of six words: three for the surname and three for the forename. What's more, the first word of the surname is "van." He simply adores surnames that begin with "van."

Why, out of the four books that the passionate reader has on his table, are two (50% exactly) Dutch? Because the Book Fair held in the city was this year devoted to Dutch literature, and that meant, on the one hand, that publishers have brought out more writers in that language recently and, on the other, that the main bookshops in the city have created special displays, piling tables up with these new books as well as books by Dutch and Flemish authors that had been published years ago, that are no longer new and were gathering dust in the distributors' warehouses.

The passionate reader has all four books in front of him and can't think where to begin. The stories by the French writer whose novel he liked several years ago? The novel by the young American about whom he knows nothing? That way, if (as is very likely) he finds it immediately disappointing, he will have eliminated one of the four at a stroke and will only have to choose from among the other three. Obviously the same may happen with the novel by the Dutch writer whom he has had to put down on two previous occasions, after merely one page. The reader opens the second book and leafs through. He opens the third and does exactly the same. And follows suit with the fourth. He could choose on the basis of the typeface or kind of paper . . . He tries to find another aspect of the books that could decide for him (an isolated sentence, a character's name). Page layout. Or paragraphing, for example. He knows that many writers struggle to create frequent paragraphs, whether the text calls for it or not, because they think that when the reader sees the page isn't too dense, he will feel better disposed toward the book. The same goes for dialogue. A serrated text, with lots of dialogue, is (according to current norms) a plus for most people. This may generally be the case, but has the opposite effect on this reader: he finds an abundance of new paragraphs irritating. He is prejudiced against, and mirrors the prejudice felt by lovers of abundant paragraphs, who find a lack of paragraphs extremely monotonous or arrogant.

Where *should* he begin? The solution might be to begin them all at once, as he often does. Not simultaneously, of course: but going from one to another, just as you never watch six TV channels at the same time but flick from one to another. Obviously there must always be a book he opens first where he reads a paragraph, a story, a chapter, twenty percent of the pages before moving on to the next. The problem is not knowing where to start. He gets up and lights a cigarette. Why is lighting up a solution when one doesn't know what to do? Lighting up shows we are thinking something through, are meditating intensely, are remembering, are waiting for someone (every so often we will draw back the curtain and look down the street) or are losing patience (in a maternity hospital waiting-room, its floor covered in cigarette butts). One enjoys a post-coital cigarette; one lights a cigarette to extinguish it in the groin of a masochist lover and increase their arousal. One lights a cigarette in search of inspiration, because the nicotine helps to stop us from dozing off, or so we don't eat when we are hungry and can't or don't want to. The passionate reader has one last drag and goes back to the table. The four books are there and, next to them, the plastic bag bearing the bookshop's red logo. Night falls; a car drives by; a radio blasts out. Do you hear a lot of radios in novels? If the four books were to disappear all of a sudden, his problem would disappear with them: where to begin? He picks up the novel by the American. He opens it to the first page. He sticks his finger forcefully between the two leaves, to keep it open, and reads: "At the very moment the nurse pulls the sheet up to cover his face, the dead man opens his eyes and whispers incoherently. The nurse screams, drops the sheet, says the patient's name, and takes his pulse. She runs out to find the doctor. 'Doctor, the patient in 114 isn't dead!' 'What do you mean, he's not dead?' 'He's not dead. He opened his eyes. I took his pulse . . .' The doctor tries to hide the unease that this piece of news provokes in him."

The reader closes the book. The first sentence, the first paragraph, the first page. The possibilities are immense, as ever. Everything still has to fan out, gradually, as the paths at the beginning fade until finally (that is, on the final page) only one remains, that is generally predictable. Will the writer keep us entranced to the last page? Won't there ever be a time, from here to the fifth, eighteenth, or one-hundred-and-sixty-seventh page when his spell will be broken. But a narrative is never as good as the possibilities that fan out at the beginning. Anyway, it's not about the reader foreseeing every possible development and improving on the ones offered by the author. No way. How would he continue the story of the man reading the newspaper in the lobby of the Ambassade Hotel who doesn't react when they shout out his name? It is that moment of indecision, when the chips are down, that attracts him. The exposition vaguely reminds him of that Hitchcock film when Cary Grant is mistaken for another man in a hotel lobby. But he's not interested in taking that thought further. To write the next scene, whatever that might be, would open the way to imperfection.

Writers err when they develop their initial expositions. They shouldn't. They should systematically set out their opening gambits and abandon them at the most enthralling point. Isn't that so with everything? Of course it is! Not only in books, but also in films or plays. Or politics. If you are ingenuous enough to believe any of that, isn't a party's political program a thousand times more interesting, positive, and stirring than its execution once the party is elected to govern? Everything is idyllic about the program. In practice, nothing is respected, everything is falsified; reality imposes its own corrosive cruelties. And (in life outside of books) isn't the beginning of love, the first look, the first kiss much richer than what comes later, that inevitably turns everything into failure? Things should always begin and never continue. Isn't a man's life enormously rich in possibilities at the age of three? What will become of this boy who is just starting out? And as he grows, life will wither everything: few of his expectations will be fulfilled, and that's if he is lucky. But just as a passionate reader cannot stop life unless he decides to cut it short, he *can* stop his books at their moment of greatest splendor, when the potential is still almost infinite. That's why it is never-ending. He only reads the beginnings, the first pages at most. When the forking paths fanning out at the start of a story begin to fade and the book is beginning to bore him, he puts it down and places it on the corresponding shelf, according to the alphabetical order of the writer's surname.

Disappointment can come at any time. In the first paragraph, on page thirty-eight, or on the penultimate page. He once reached the last page of a book. He was about to begin the last paragraph (a short paragraph, about a third of a page), and hadn't yet been disappointed, when he took fright. What if that book didn't disappoint—even in the last line? It was altogether improbable; you simply know disappointment had to set in, if only with the last word, as it always did. But what if it didn't? Just in case, he quickly looked away, five lines from that final full stop. He closed the book, put it back in its place, and took a deep breath; that demonstration of his willpower allows him to continue fantasizing that sooner or later (on the most unlikely day, the moment *he* finally does decide), he will have the courage to stop eternally deferring a decision that is final.

Quim Monzó was born in Barcelona in 1952. He has been awarded the National Award, the City of Barcelona Award, the Prudenci Bertrana Award, the El Temps Award, the Lletra d'Or Prize for the best book of the year, and the Catalan Writers' Award, and he has abeen awarded *Serra d'Or* magazine's prestigious Critics' Award four times. He has also translated numerous authors into Catalan, including Truman Capote, J. D. Salinger, and Ernest Hemingway.

Peter Bush is a renowned translator from Catalan, French, Spanish, and Portuguese. He has translated such writers as Juan Goytisolo, Leonardo Padura, and Luis Sepúlveda, and was awarded the Valle-Inclán Literary Translation Prize for his translation of Goytisolo's *The Marx Family Saga*. He is currently visiting professor at the University of Málaga.

Open Letter—the University of Rochester's nonprofit, literary translation press—is one of only a handful of publishing houses dedicated to increasing access to world literature for English readers. Publishing ten titles in translation each year, Open Letter searches for works that are extraordinary and influential, works that we hope will become the classics of tomorrow.

Making world literature available in English is crucial to opening our cultural borders, and its availability plays a vital role in maintaining a healthy and vibrant book culture. Open Letter strives to cultivate an audience for these works by helping readers discover imaginative, stunning works of fiction and by creating a constellation of international writing that is engaging, stimulating, and enduring.

Current and forthcoming titles from Open Letter include works from Argentina, Catalonia, China, Czech Republic, Poland, Russia, and numerous other countries.

www.openletterbooks.org